Watching Charlotte Brontë Die:

and other surreal stories

Also by Ellie Stevenson

Ship of Haunts: the other Titanic Story (novel)

For more information on Ellie Stevenson and her
work see:

www.elliestevenson.co.uk
http://elliestevenson.wordpress.com

Watching Charlotte Brontë Die:

and other surreal stories

Ellie Stevenson

Rosegate Publications

First published in 2013 by Rosegate Publications

ISBN 978-0-9572165-3-2

Image © iStockphoto.com
Cover design by James Allwright

Watching Charlotte Brontë Die:

and other surreal stories

CONTENTS

Unexpected News

Dorothy Taylor breathed in dust like it was her own, her own worn bones being ground into dirt. Instead of being just a tired old floor, and hardly dirty, she'd swept it herself. Such a pity her head was pressed up against it.

She could feel Jack's foot in the small of her back, could smell his shoes, and something else, the smell of old sock. She was surprised that Jack could afford leather shoes, he was only part-time, and when he was here he worked so little. And then she smelt something worse than socks, sweat and fear. She got to her feet as Jack released her, watched him leave, finally cowed, as bullies always were when they met someone bigger. The person in question was Alison Beaumont, she *was* bigger, *and* also had the ear of the man in charge. Dorothy groaned.

Alison Beaumont was normally sharp but today the woman looked dulled with grief. Dorothy noticed the flash of her eyes and guessed the grief might come with a spark. The woman was angry, very angry.

'Get me some tea, Doris,' she said.

Beaumont never remembered her name, but today was not a day to argue. Dorothy sighed and left the room, following Jack into the corridor and then to the staffroom. When she got back, Alison Beaumont was by the window and staring out of the grimy panes.

'These all need a clean,' she said to Dot, running a finger down the glass, which came away smudged with grease and dirt. She looked surprised.

Dorothy didn't bother to answer, *she* was a carer, it wasn't *her* job to clean the windows. But the Home cared less about people than money, and not having cleaners saved quite a bit. Dorothy knew she ought to tell, but also knew she never would. She needed the pay.

Alison Beaumont sniffed and sat down. 'I've come to see you about my mother. Now that she's dead.'

Old Annie Barton was better than you, thought Dot savagely, grief surprising her with its appearance. A small, hollow pain was birthed in her gut. *At least your mother, Annie, was kind.*

Alison Beaumont leant towards her. 'My mother left you a small legacy.' The frown on her face was comment enough and pure displeasure, that and the stress on the word *small*. But Dot didn't care, the round, hollow pain was replaced by pride. Dot was in a fantasy world.

What would it be, this *small* legacy? A simple gift, some flowers or a vase? Maybe money, but not that much. A little something to make a difference. She hardly dared hope.

Alison Beaumont pursed her lips. 'You needn't look like that,' she said. 'My mother left you a garden shed.'

Dorothy stared at herself in the mirror. Her eyes were small and her nose was big, far too big for the size of her face, but somehow, today, that didn't matter. She adjusted the mirror, which wouldn't stay straight, no matter how many times she tried. Dorothy frowned. The mirror was tired and old, like her, or so she felt, but it hung there proud in the tiny shed. She'd never had *anything* like a shed. Living in a tiny, top floor flat, she'd never even had so much as a yard. And now she had her very own shed. It even came with electric light. *How strange*, she thought.

'I still remember when Annie's old man wired the place,' said Artie Frost, the elderly neighbour, who lived next door. They'd met across the garden fence. 'I doubt it would pass the safety tests, not then or now. He was always one for DIY, was my mate Eddie.'

Dorothy nodded, she didn't care much about DIY and Eddie Barton, not right then, she was cold and tired and needed some heat. She thought there might be a mystery here, electric lights and the missing man, but she knew it would keep, for now was December, and the leaves on the trees, so lovely once, had dropped to the ground and turned to mush.

'Just like your meals,' said Ralph, her bloke, a fly-by-night type, but all she could get. Dorothy thought he was probably married, but she didn't dare ask and he wasn't going to say. He never had any money either.

Dorothy sighed and thought of the shed. It wasn't exactly a normal gift and the garden belonged to someone else.

'It's a pity she didn't leave you the house,' said Ralph shortly, poking the fire.

'Isn't it just,' said Dot, sadly.

When she returned to the house after Christmas, she took the time, and examined it properly. The street was fat and clearly prosperous, with tall, broad houses and buffed up steps. All except one, old Annie Barton's, it looked rather shabby. She let herself through by the garden gate.

The windows were shuttered and closed to the world. The house looked grim, in need of improvement, the garden was worse. Dot feared gardens, their untamed nature and the secret rules she'd never managed to learn. According to Artie, there'd once been a lawn and beautiful plants *and* a brand new shed. It was hard to believe. 'He left just after he fitted the electrics,' Artie explained, speaking of Eddie, 'just packed up his bags, and left, like that.' He clicked his fingers, a sharp, twanging sound that symbolised loss.

Dot said nothing, just smiled slightly, she'd taken to Artie, who'd become more generous, sharing gossip and bits of news.

'You know she's putting the house on the market?'

Dorothy nodded, she hadn't known but she'd guessed as much, it was obvious, really. The house was empty and rather run down, but still substantial, a valuable asset, and Alison Beaumont wasn't the type to waste an asset. A few days later, the woman herself turned up at the shed.

'I rather thought I'd find you here.'

'It makes a change,' said Dot, mildly. 'From the Home, I mean. Would you like some tea? The kettle's just on.'

'In *here*?' said Alison Beaumont rudely, scanning the space with her sharp, black eyes. She seemed to think the idea crazy, but squeezed herself in and perched on a chair.

'You've made the place look almost homely. I only came to give you this.'

This was a box tied up with string. It was long and narrow and opened easily.

'It's an easel,' said Dot, pleased but surprised. She hadn't expected Annie to remember.

'I think it's why she gave you the shed.' Alison Beaumont tapped the box. 'I found it when I was clearing up.'

'She always knew I wanted to paint. And now she's given me something towards it. Two things really.' A shaft of light hit the grimy panes and a thousand colours entered the room. 'I always thought she'd forgotten,' she said.

'My mother never forgot *anything*,' Alison Beaumont, said with feeling. 'Not bad tea, for *you*, Doris.'

'My name's Dot,' said Dorothy, sharply.

Alison Beaumont put the mug down. 'You know I'm selling the house, don't you?'

'I thought you would,' said Dot sadly. 'But of course I'm sorry.'

'You've made this place look *so* much better, all those prints and that lovely old rug. And the lights still work, my Dad did those.'

'Yes,' said Dorothy, drifting off, to a much better place of landscape oils and vibrant hues.

'He really was rather good, you know, at that sort of thing.'

'What?' said Dorothy, coming back, but rather reluctant.

'My Dad, Doris. He loved model trains and he liked a smoke. Mother wouldn't let him smoke in the house, so he built this shed and moved in here. He used to spend all his time in here, turned it into a home from home.' She paused briefly. 'Rather like you, without the trains.'

'Right,' said Dorothy, looking around and wondering where the trains would have gone.

Alison Beaumont reached in her coat and pulled out a packet of cigarettes. 'Want one?' she said.

Dorothy shook her head sharply, wondering how to say, 'Not here. This is *my* shed now.'

But Alison Beaumont didn't argue, just shoved the packet back in her pocket and carried on talking. 'My mother never believed he'd left, would leave all this, apart from her.' She looked outside at the overgrown garden. Dorothy looked for somewhere to go.

'He wasn't really my Dad, you know.' Alison Beaumont got to her feet.

'Right,' said Dot. What could she say?

'She should have had the thing knocked down, the moment he left.' Alison Beaumont's voice was harsh. She walked to the door, then looked at Dot. 'My mother always hoped he'd come back. And now the wretched shed is yours.'

Weeks passed and a thaw came on, and working outside in the early evenings became almost possible. Dot spent time in the garden, painting.

'I reckon you've got a bloke down there,' said Ralph, moaning.

'You're probably right,' said Dot mildly, thinking of Artie. 'He's quite debonair, and much more polite than you'll ever be.'

Ralph didn't answer, just snorted loudly and made for the door. Dot was joking but Ralph didn't see it, he was far too angry. He left for the pub, slamming the door as hard as he could. Dorothy sighed. Things weren't great at home, these days.

It wasn't much better at the shed either. However she tried, she couldn't quite get the shapes right on the sketches she made, or catch the mists of seasonal rain. All her paintings looked indifferent. *I'll never be any good at this*, she thought, sadly.

A few weeks later, the weather improved, but the painting hadn't. Buds emerged but Dot couldn't draw them, leaves looked wrong. Artie appeared across the fence.

'Still painting I see,' he said smiling and Dorothy nodded.

'I try,' she said, 'but it won't work out.'

Artie climbed over and studied her latest effort closely. 'I reckon you're trying to do too much, at least for now. You need to focus on something smaller. Try those anemones over there.'

'Do you think that's it?' said Dorothy, hopeful, looking at the plant, which was small and pretty but mostly weeds.

'I do,' he said, as the rain came down and soaked them both as well as her painting.

'Oh, look, it's ruined,' said Dot fed up, 'and the shed'll be wet and the lights'll go off. I'm sure those electrics aren't safe, you know, just like you said. It's not that I'm not grateful, though.' Her voice trailed off.

'I know you are,' said Artie, nodding 'I know you are.' He looked thoughtful.

'Why don't I give you the key to the house? The power's still on in there, I think, and at least it's dry. It's a better place to paint than out here, or in that shed.'

'What? Annie's old house? I don't think so.'

'But who's to know bar you and me? I've had that key for years,' he said. 'I got it from Annie, in case of trouble. Not many people know I've got it.'

Dot knew he meant Alison Beaumont, *she* wouldn't want her going inside. But old Annie Barton had been her friend, and Dorothy wanted to see the place, just once.

'I shouldn't really,' she said, weakening.

'It'll be alright,' Artie insisted. 'And I'll come with you, just this first time, so you'll know it's safe. Let's go now.'

'Right' said Dot, knowing it was wrong, but following Artie down the path, he was miles ahead and rushing with the vigour of a much younger man. Dorothy followed him into the house. The hall was huge.

'Better not switch the lights on yet,' said Artie, laughing. 'God knows what we'll see in here.'

They wandered around from room to room, looking at curtains closed to the light, and left-over furniture, covered in sheets.

'Nobody's been in here for years,' said Dot with feeling. 'Look at the dust, it's inches thick.'

'No-one apart from Alison Beaumont. And I don't think she's the cleaning sort.'

The word *cleaning* leapt out at Dorothy, swung from a thread, was hung out to dry. Like rags and cloths and freshly washed curtains. 'No,' she said, and wandered away. After that, the rest was easy. *I'm doing it all for Annie*, she thought. But she knew it was all for herself and the house.

As they left she turned to Artie. 'Did you know my friend Annie well?' she asked, curious.

Artie took a moment to answer. 'In some ways, yes, I did, very well. But in others, no, hardly at all. Nor her, me.'

Then the lights came on in the street outside.

The season took hold, got into its swing, and all the gardens were bright with colour. Annie's old neighbour, Artie Frost, was bored with hanging around his house, so he wandered next door, and let himself in with his duplicate key. He stopped, stunned. The house was still cold and empty, yes. But the floors had been polished, the windows gleamed and someone had taken the dustsheets off. The house was different, had a sort of glow, just like it had then, in Annie's day. Artie smiled, he knew the touch of a woman's heart and he thought he knew who the woman was. She walked towards him, down the hall.

'I thought I heard your footsteps just now, you gave me a fright.' Artie grinned, she didn't look scared.

'I see you've been busy in here, my girl. The place looks great, you've done a good job.' Dorothy scowled.

'My bloke's left home, I needed something different to do, apart from the job. Something to keep my mind off Ralph.' She looked defiant, not at all sad.

Artie smiled, he didn't believe a word she'd said. He'd seen the glint that lit her eye, that very first day. Perhaps that's why he'd asked her here. But what would Alison Beaumont say?

Then he heard the key in the lock.

'Time to go,' he said shortly, and scuttled away as fast as he could. Leaving Dorothy far behind. He'd always avoided Annie's daughter.

Alison Beaumont looked outraged and so she might. 'What do you think you're doing in here?'

Dorothy grasped the vacuum firmly. She might as well be hung for a sheep...

'I thought I'd do it for Annie,' she said.

'But how did you get inside the house?' She paused briefly. 'It's sold by the way, the agent gave me the news this morning. They've even paid more for your wretched shed.' Her eyes glowed. 'You know you're breaking the law don't you?'

'But Artie Frost gave me the key.' Dorothy swore, and clapped her hand over her mouth. She hadn't meant to mention Artie.

'Yeah, sure he did. I remember him, a right layabout, never at work. Him and my father were thick as thieves. Eddie wasn't my father, you know.'

'Yes, you said,' Dot nodded, feeling weary, but thinking rapidly. *If Eddie wasn't, who was?* Thoughts of Artie slipped into her mind, a man perhaps once sweet on Annie, a man who might have been Alison's father. It could be true. Maybe that's why he'd lent her the key.

Dorothy considered. It was hard to tell, with him being old, but Beaumont's look matched his to a tee. She couldn't ask but she wished she could.

Alison Beaumont hurried her out, slamming the door, and turning the key with extra force.

'Just one more thing,' she said sharply, grabbing her arm, as she sailed down the path. 'I know your work probably helped with the sale, and for that I'm grateful. We'll leave it there, on one condition.'

Dot waited.

'I heard what you said about Artie Frost, and I know it's not true. Where did you really get that key?'

13

'Where I said, from the man next door.' Dorothy felt annoyed and tired. Did the woman never listen?

'No you didn't,' said Alison Beaumont. 'Try again, I know it's a lie. Artie Frost's been dead for years.'

Anna Grail

I'll never forget when Tom Lowe left me. That was the day the gatepost collapsed and Mother had to fix it with string. Well, tights, actually, but who's looking? I only hope she washed them first. Oh, and the rest. It was Valentine's Day.

'You're fat, Anna Grail,' said Tom with a sigh. 'I can't go out with a lump, not anymore. There are far better fish to fry around here.' I heard his words, but I didn't believe him, there were six hundred people on the whole island, that's not a lot of choice, when you take off the men, the old and the married. But I didn't say so. I knew from his face, he'd made up his mind.

His words hurt, we'd been together for about six months, that's almost an engagement in our little landscape. What hurt most of all were the expectations, not mine so much, as other peoples: *where, when, and will you make sure I catch the bouquet?* And worst of all: *Isn't Tom lucky?* But Tom thought luck was getting out fast.

'Never you mind,' my mother said, when I told her the news, later that evening. 'There're plenty more men where that one came from.' I didn't agree – I thought my chances were exceedingly slim. Unlike me. It was time to take stock.

I needed to find a different life. Girls my age, when they split with a bloke, got drunk, got silly, then went out shopping and bought a new dress. None of those things would work for me. I needed something more than frivolous, maybe drastic. Perhaps I needed a reinvention.

Two weeks later I was sitting in the pub (we've only the one) and Tom came in, with Jessica Saddle on his arm. She was the one who drove the carriages round the island, showing off the sights as well as herself. I gritted my teeth when I saw her walk in. She's a good looking girl, is Jessica Saddle, but I know my Tom, it's money he likes and the Saddles had money, shed loads of it. And not just cash but land as well, all over the place. Now, I'm not stupid, I can drive a tractor, there aren't any cars on the whole island, and tractor driving is almost essential, but I don't have money, not even a piggybank. Mother always hoped I'd marry a farmer, but farmers are scarce and usually taken, and as it happens, I work in the shop. Shop work's ok, and the discount's handy, but it's not exactly a road to the stars.

'You look at Rosalie-Ann,' said my mother. 'She married the Prince lad, the youngest boy, and now her kids are heirs to a fortune.' I sighed loudly.

Life can be hard when you disappoint yourself, but it's ten times worse when Mother pays the bill.

Later that night I was surfing the web, playing an argument back in my head, with Tom, of course. I still remember how it went.

'Broadband?' said Tom. 'Why would a girl like you want Broadband? The web's alright for city types, but not for folk who live around here.' I glanced at the screen.

'It's fast,' I said. 'You can go where you like and see what you like, without even leaving the comfort of home. And it doesn't cost more, once you're on.'

'Ha!' said Tom, as he leant across and switched off the screen. 'I'm not having you neglecting me, all for a bloke who's not really there, who's probably enhanced.'

Ha! indeed. Those were the days when he thought he loved me.

Months later, there I was, but the joys of surfing the web had faded. I was bored and fed up, I needed a change. I clicked on a link. And read the text.

Need hope, happiness, or a new career? Perhaps you'd like to improve your life?

Seen a great job but don't have the words? We can help you win that position.

Fill in our form and you'll succeed.

Do it now.

Applications are Us

Ok, I thought. So that's what I did.

Admin assistant Melanie Jones was sitting at her desk. She was bored and restless and playing with her hair, twisting gold strands around her fingers. She sighed heavily and glanced across at the man opposite.

'Three more forms have just come in,' she said to her colleague. 'One from some place in the middle of nowhere. God knows why she'd even bother.' She threaded paperclips into a chain. 'Who do want me to be today?'

Martyn, the manager, raised his head. 'I've told you Mel, be anyone you want. But I gave you the list; today's Thursday.'

'Ok, ok, I was only asking,' Melanie frowned and studied the sheet. 'I think for a change, I'll be

Alice instead. You know, like Alice in Wonderland.'

Martyn grunted and went on typing. The click of the keys was fast and loud. He didn't spare her another glance, didn't even raise his head from his work. Melanie sighed and stared at her screen. Her fingers danced across the keyboard.

Dear Anna – thanks for your form. One of our team will be in touch. Send us the details of the job you want and we'll write the form to your requirements. If you've any more questions, just get in touch.

Kind regards

Alice Smith (Customer Services)
Applications are Us

Melanie smiled and read the email a second time. She quickly and deftly removed the last line. She didn't want Anna to have any questions, questions meant problems and Melanie Jones liked an easy life. Mel sighed. She certainly didn't have one here.

A click of the mouse and the message was gone, wizzing its way across the ether. She leant across and grabbed her mug, the one with the chip. As she got up, the pc bleeped. *Damn*, thought

Melanie, *more wretched orders*. She checked the screen.

'You've got a few more,' she said to Martyn. 'The first one's a doddle, but look out for the second, he sounds like a prat. He's something big in Engineering. Can't say I like it.'

'Just as well you're not the one who's doing it, then,' said Martyn sourly.

Melanie frowned and made for the door. This sure was some weird job.

Three weeks later

It was early on Monday, dark for the time, and the sea looked grey and very forbidding. That was ok, *I* was used to bad weather. Rough crossings were normal to me. There were only four of us on the boat, and I was standing outside on my own. The door opened and Davin appeared, two old hands alone in the squall. The boat rose and dropped like a stone, and my stomach dropped with it. Then we got wet. Davin laughed.

'Not like you to be up this early,' he said, smiling. Everyone knew I stayed up late, surfing the web.

'I'm off to London to seek my fortune.' Forever, I hoped, not that I said so. Davin sniffed, he didn't approve.

'You'll not be happy there,' he said. 'No green fields or tractors in London.'

'No,' I said. 'But I'm not that happy here, right now.'

Davin sighed and turned away. He'd heard about Jessica Saddle, of course. I'd heard he used to like her himself. 'You can always come back,' he said gruffly, from beneath his coat. His words were muffled, I could hardly hear. 'In a few months time, when things settle down. Not everything lasts, at least not forever.' We stared out to sea.

I wondered if I'd have Tom back, if I could. I didn't know. I stood there thinking, toying with the ticket I had in my pocket. I'd bought a return, just in case. But I wasn't saying.

Three days later, I felt exhausted, having done the rounds of all the employers, having dragged myself through soulless streets. My feet felt leaden, there were no gold pavements, only cement. And jobs, jobs, jobs.

'Too young,' said the first.

'Too old,' said the second.

'Not nearly enough experience, *my dear*' said the third, fourth and fifth.

The sixth one I tried was a bit more constructive. 'Have you thought about getting a job in a shop?' said the manager kindly. His smile looked sad.

'Have you thought about getting some help with your form?' said the seventh, and last.

The telephone rang. 'Applications are Us,' said Melanie, shortly.

'I want to complain,' said the voice on the phone. It was male, middle-aged, with a civil servant's quality, stuffy and proud and very well paid. *Too* well paid, Martyn had said.

'Sorry,' said Melanie, chewing on a nail. She didn't feel sorry.

'Sorry won't make my form look right,' said the grumpy old git, as he coughed and wheezed his way down the phone. 'You've changed it so often it sounds like a stranger's. And you still don't know how to spell *advancement*.'

So choose another word, thought Melanie sharply, but she kept her crazy thoughts to herself.

'I want someone else to work on my form, do you hear me sweetheart? I've paid good money and I want your top man. I want someone different.'

There is no-one different, thought Melanie grimly. There's only me and the Wizard of Oz. She wondered how to get rid of the bloke.

'I hear you Sir,' she said sweetly, her voice full of sugar, or maybe poison. 'You want our top man to work on your form. Just leave it with me.'

Our only man, she said to herself as she put down the phone. And he was the one who did it before.

The other phone rang and Melanie swore as she glanced at her watch and noticed the time. It was almost two and Martyn *still* wasn't back from lunch. *Where the hell had he got to this time?* she wondered. She put down the phone on another client, some kind of teacher, and grabbing her bag, made for the door. If she didn't go now she'd miss her chance for the job in Chelsea. *Damn Martyn, damn everyone.*

Melanie hurried along the road, as fast as she could, pulling off her shoes, her bright red heels. 'Taxi,' she yelled, yelling for a pipe dream. 'Taxi! Taxi!' She thought she saw something, a big black cab but it sailed right past. She didn't see the girl who was shorter and fatter and right in her way. Until they collided.

Melanie shrieked and fell to the pavement, scattering her handbag's contents all over. She glared at the girl who'd caused all the trouble.

'Sorry,' the girl said, looking embarrassed. She started picking up Melanie's things but Melanie didn't have time to wait. She grabbed her shoes, her bag, and whatever, and dragged herself up and along the street. She still had time to make it, maybe…

A few minutes later, bedraggled and weary, Anna stood outside Martyn's office. Assorted creatives hung around chatting, laughing and joking and leaning on walls. Anna ignored them. She pushed on the door, which, surprisingly, opened and found herself inside the building. The office was small, just two tiny rooms, divided by chipboard, with one small window. The first room she entered held two large desks but both of the rooms were empty of staff. The phone started ringing. She picked up the handset.

'Applications are Us,' she said, brightly, looking at the logo. 'How can I help?'

'I very much doubt you can young lady. Nobody seems to listen to me. Not even you, though I pay you to.'

'But I don't even work here, Sir' said Anna. 'I've just walked in.'

'So you all say,' said the man, sourly. 'I suppose that's why you answered the phone.'

Anna said nothing, he did have a point.

'I tell you what,' she said smiling, hoping her smile could be heard in her voice. 'Why don't you tell me what's gone wrong. Then, later, I can pass on the message.' She'd charm this man, the way she had Tom. *It's only a game,* she said to herself.

The man grunted, he wanted to talk. 'What did you say your name was love?'

Hell, thought Anna, *he wants my name.* Maybe this wasn't such a good idea. She looked at the sheet on the desk beside her. It was definitely Thursday.

'Barbara,' she said. 'My name's Barbara.'

The door opened and a man walked in, looking distracted. When he saw Anna his expression changed from distraction to anger. 'What do you think you're doing in here?' he said, sharply. He strode across to where she was standing, grabbed the phone and slammed it back down.

'I was talking to someone,' said Anna stiffly, watching him do his little dance. 'One of your customers, as it happens.'

'Moaners, you mean, that's what they are. Always complaining. And who are you?'

'Barbara,' she said,' or rather, I'm Anna. Anna Grail. I've come for my form, for the job in Camden. It's been over three weeks, almost four.'

'You're supposed to ring, or send an email. We don't have a shop front service here.'

'I did,' said Anna, 'I did both of those, but nobody answered. I've waited so long the post's been filled. I didn't even bother to apply myself, I've been hanging around waiting for you. And now I've paid you money for nothing, and I'm still unemployed. And I thought *you* were supposed to help.'

The man didn't answer straight away, just ran his fingers through dirty blonde hair. He looked harassed. 'I'm afraid things have been in a bit of a mess. My assistant, Mel...' He looked around.

'She seems to have vanished.' The phone rang again.

Anna stared, but just for a moment. She picked up the handset. 'Applications are Us,' she said, smoothly. But the smile had gone.

'My assistant Mel,' said Martyn, later, 'she'll have the details of your application. Melanie deals with all the admin. Or, at least, she's supposed to.' He sighed, frustrated and looked at his watch. 'I can't imagine where she is.'

'She wouldn't be a blonde in a smart red dress, with bright red shoes? I bumped into someone like that earlier. She was definitely going in the opposite direction. And running like mad.'

Martyn nodded. 'That sounds like Mel, always in a hurry, but not to come here. I tell you Anna, the girl's hopeless. She might have looks, but her brain's like mush. She couldn't even tell me what her name was today.'

They both laughed.

'About your form,' said Martyn, thinking. 'I'm sure we could fix it, given some time. Why don't you stay here, answer the phone, 'til Mel gets back, and then we'll see.' He looked hopeful. 'What do you say?'

Anna smiled. She doubted Mel was coming back, today or ever. But, more to the point, should *she* stay? Maybe she should, she'd nowhere better to go right now and if she did, she could always leave, whenever she wanted. She felt in her pocket for her ticket home, that tiny piece of warmth, security. It wasn't there. She must have lost it when she fell. Anna sighed. The decision was made. The phone rang. 'Applications are Us,' said Anna firmly. 'Barbara speaking.'

Martyn and I bought a farm in Surrey. Mother was pleased, she thought the farm meant I'd finally arrived, and I was pleased because at last it meant I could drive a tractor, whenever I wanted. Once I'd persuaded Martyn to get one, and hire some staff to run the business. It all went fine.

I kept in touch with island gossip, through Davin mostly. He'd always been a bit soft on me, despite his thing about Jessica Saddle. We were both amused by the latest news. Jessica Saddle had dumped Tom, and not as you'd think, for a man with a farm, but for somebody new, and a girl at that, a mystery stranger from the mainland. Tall, blonde and very good-looking. Somebody said she wore bright red shoes.

Tom was stunned, but I wasn't. It just went to show what Mother said, over and over.

'Letting you go was Tom Lowe's downfall. He's bound to regret it.'

Room Forty-Two

Forty-two. The meaning of life? No, it's a number, leading to a room, a room that doesn't exist anymore. The smoking room.

Before the ban, before smoking wasn't allowed, one of our colleges had such a room, a room just for them, the people who smoked.

Empty, white; white, milk of magnesia walls, oozing into sludge. The soft, squat chairs, speaking of loss, control abandoned, shabby split covers, and soft loose parts, old-curry brown. A hated room. She goes there to meet my lover.

Sometimes I hover, waiting at the edge, like some sort of angel, nobody wants. Eyes darting, through a haze of smoke, cigarette smoke, listening for laughter, wanting to hear it, wanting not. And in the end, there's only the clink, cup upon cup, all of that coffee, friends meeting friends, for a drink or a chat. Something I know nothing about.

Sometimes she's a demon, prowling the passages, looking for my lover, my partner in crime, who's mine to lust for. Sometimes I'm shocked by her pale pink face, her baby blue eyes, her soft chiselled voice, someone so real she can't be the devil. But the devil here comes well disguised. And now they've taken the paintings down, to auction for cash, to keep this place of learning alive. Well I'm learning, without the cash, without the course, and it's not a lesson I want to learn. She goes in there to meet my lover.

I stare at the room without its paintings. The walls beneath, less white, not more, as if the paintings were just a cover, hiding the green and gold of it all. When the coffee has gone and the people too. A room alive.

Early morning is when I come here, the breaking dawn splits the room in two, light and dark, gold and green. I creep in then, and take possession. Stand alone, on the carpet tiles, absorb the thoughts, the feelings of others. It's my room then. And just for a moment, I relent a little, decide the room's not bad after all, with its cracks in the paintwork, its old chipped door. Even the stains on the glass have charm.

One thing's the same, dawn or dusk, the cigarette smell of furtive moments, a secret vice that all of them share. Moved to a room, away from the rest, to have their break: it ought to be some sort of exclusion. Instead it's become a secret club. Where my lover lives, enjoys, rejoices, shares his life with his special friends. I wait by the door, peer through the glass, squint through the gap when someone goes in. Room forty-two, the smoker's room, the place I can only go on my own. I can barely see, through the haze of the smell, barely breathe, even at the door. But I know she's in there, laughing and talking, simpering even, enjoying his time. She goes in there at least twice a day, to meet my lover.

And worst of all, she doesn't even smoke.

The Window Box

Got under my skin. That's what you did. And not in a good way.

When I was six I was playing on the streets, we all did then. It was a halcyon time, before mass-produced traffic and the threat of paedophiles on every corner. The dangerous people were those we knew.

I was playing, I was running, and then I fell. I screamed and cried – of course I did, I was only six. My hands were grazed, with blood and stone and shards of glass, embossing the surface of my skin. I ran home at once, or to what I called home, my stepmother, Katie.

She, Katie, took out all the stones with a pair of tweezers. Bits of flint and strips of glass. But she didn't manage to remove it all. There was one piece left, sharp and lethal. That was you.

Years later, I still bear the scars. I never told Katie I was running away from you when I fell. That I was running away from your long dark hair, and your wide-eyed smile, and your cold, cruel heart. I couldn't run far. I still can't.

Our alley was like the ones in the photos, the ones with washing across the lane and the children playing in gaps in between. Ducking and diving beneath the covers. In those prints, the washing is always pure and clean, the alleys are always wide and empty. The photos are sepia, stripping away the dirt and the pain. If I look at those photos carefully enough, I can see myself as I was then. Playing in the shadows.

I stare outside, through a large sash window. My house is tall, three storeys high, with my favourite room, a workroom for sewing, right at the top. Outside the window is a broad stone ledge, perfect for plants. I run my hands over its surface, like the palms of my hands once ran over you. You were always the leader and we all followed, a tiny gang, defiant and hungry, with you at its heart. *We* had a blood pact, you and I. You ripped the skin on my quivering thumb with a sharp grey stone, and made it bleed. Then you pressed your thumb, hard, into mine. There was no romance, only intent. The smell of the drains rose up from the gutters and mingled with sweat. I was younger then, only five, but already lost. Bikes sailed past, kids in the air, and balls lay on the pavement, waiting. They were waiting for a game, but there weren't any games, not for me, there was only you. You and you, and only you. And now, we're both lost.

On the ledge outside my window is a window box, it's stuffed with plants, a riot of colour, crimson and cinnamon, violet and blue. Every season the flowers change, but come the winter, the box stands empty, apart from the ivy which lasts so well. Last year I thought I'd try holly for a change, a vibrant green and shiny red berries, but, despite my efforts, it didn't really take. I preferred the blue, it suited my mood.

As I grew up on our dirty back streets, my back became straighter and my hair longer. I was tall for my age, tall for a girl and too tall for you. We were 15 then, and you started seeing somebody else, a girl from round here, she was rich and clean. In less than a year, you dropped the girl and decided you'd try a boy instead. He was fit and cool and nice as well, but he was just a diversion. We both knew it.

At seventeen there were girls again, an assortment of colours, slanty-eyed witches, dripping their lips all over your skin. I hated them all, wanted to kill them, but held myself back. Not one of them knows you like me, I thought.

The window box on the broad stone ledge is also of stone. It moves easily, with a bit of a push but it's fairly solid. Dangerous when falling, three storeys would do it. I tell myself that there comes a time when it's harder to live with love than without. When even the sight of a street or a house, laced with memories, is too much to bear. And there are *so* many memories.

I was 21 and working in a shop, when you finally claimed me. We had given up the streets but the call of those days lived on in our blood and more besides. You still lodged with your mother in a terrace, and worked at the factory, tied to a lathe. I lived with Dad and stepmother Katie – Mother had vanished years before. I think she'd thought my father would die of a broken heart, but he didn't die, not then at least, he took up with Kate. She was round and soft and beautiful besides and she wasn't good at being my mother, being young and careless and mostly indifferent, but her careless ways were tempered with kindness, and that was enough.

Years later, when you'd claimed me and homed me and left me again, my father turned up in the middle of the night.

'She's gone,' he said, looking bereft.

'Who?' I asked, pushing my hair away from my face. It was four in the morning and my body was tired, my brain was half dead.

'Katie,' he said and started to cry.

I couldn't believe it. Katie and Father were two of a kind, she'd stuck by him through the worst of the catcalls, nobody liked him being older than her. A lot older. Then I heard who she'd left Dad for, and poured us both whisky, thinking I needed it more than him. For Katie had run off with you.

I'd had five brief years of living with you, glorious, wonderful, hurting years. And now you'd run off with somebody's wife, and not just anyone, no, my father. I hated you then, and not for the first time.

Katie, apparently, wanted a child. My father had me, his only offspring, or maybe he hadn't been able to perform, but you of course, were a different beast, you soon surpassed my father's efforts and before very long, Katie was pregnant, again and again. Time passed and then the factory made you redundant.

I opened the door and there she was, as pretty as ever, but thinner somehow, and all forlorn. She'd come to see my father, I think, she wanted a handout. My father, who'd moved in after her departure, was out, luckily.

'Fuck off Katie,' I said, bluntly.

'The children are starving and we've got no heat.'

'So get yourself down to the Social, then.'

She'd already tried, had been given some help. But you were too proud to take their handouts, and far too picky for labouring jobs. Arrogant, angry, resentful, as always. I thought for a while then opened my purse. Katie had almost loved me, once.

Her eyes widened when she saw the fifties. I'd done well for myself, had broken away from my back street life, had my own little business, dressmaking mostly, classy and vintage, but sold on a shoestring. Make do and mend had a whole new meaning for me these days. Sometimes fate can have the last laugh. I smiled broadly, and handed it over.

'Keep it,' I said. 'I don't need it.'

She flinched at my words, or maybe my tone, but her eyes glowed, were almost greedy, her fingers flexed as they touched the notes.

'I'll pay it back, I will, promise.'

With three children? I don't think so.

'That's for the kids,' I said, harshly. 'Not for you, and not for him, especially not for beer and fags. And don't expect me to offer again. So, don't come back.'

She looked upset as I said those words and hurried away as fast as she could. I think she thought I might change my mind.

'I'm ever so grateful.'

'Right,' I said, and slammed the door.

Then I sat down in the chair and cried. You never knew I cried, but I did.

Late last autumn I polished the sill. The window box that sat on the sill was painted red, a pillar box red, it went well with the holly. I pushed the box and it moved easily, sliding softly across smooth stone. I felt so weary, worn in heart by the long sad years when you'd kissed me and loved me, but never enough. And only when there was no-one else left. I'd thought and hoped we would leave this town, when you'd used up all the pretty young girls, but instead we stayed and I was the one who was all used up. All wrung out with sex and sweat, and the endless longing, never fulfilled. I was always stretching, reaching for something that didn't exist. Instead of your love, I developed and ran a successful business, but the shop in my heart had empty shelves. And then Katie took you, for good.

The day arrives. This house of mine, which is all my own, has a beautiful garden, a lawn in the centre, surrounded by shrubs and a tiny patio. My father likes to sit on the lawn, on his garden bench, watching the birds and the people next door. I even bought a table and chairs. Today I put several chairs in the garden, it's winter now, but mild all the same, and I tell Katie it means you can smoke.

I've waited so long and now is the time. A few years have passed since Katie came calling, her kids are older, we're all very different, Katie the most, not plump and pretty like in the old days, but tight, tense, worn down by poverty, but mostly by you.

You turn up at two, it's a perfect day – drab and dry, there's not even a wind. Katie is nervous, pliant and sorry. It's easy to imagine her biting her lip and chewing her nails, perhaps she does. It was easy to get you to agree to call, to lure you here with gifts and promises, a loan or some cash for these difficult times. I notice you're not so proud anymore. I've made you promise I'll be a godparent, for the latest arrival. As if I'd care.

'It's the least I can do for your little boy,' I say, smiling. Katie looks doubtful. I think she knows she's too old to be a mother again. She glances around, as if looking for my father, and as she does, she takes a biscuit. I've already told her he won't be here. He's not needed.

'Tea,' I say, handing out mugs from a scratched wooden tray that's already suffered a number of dents. The day is growing rapidly colder, none of us want to be outside. You take your tea, but say nothing, puff away on your French cigarettes. Since you've had Kat, you've been almost silent, sullen and terse, a mere shadow of your former self. I blame Katie, but in fact it's probably unemployment. I still care. I hate you too.

No-one can think of a thing to say, now we've discussed the price of a child. I'm vague and preoccupied, taken up with this thing I might do. I keep myself amused by handing out biscuits and discussing the weather. Katie takes another and gobbles it quickly. It really doesn't suit her, being this thin. You sit beside me, just like I asked, with Katie on the other side, feeling, no doubt, contempt or pity. All that money and still not happy.

At just after three I excuse myself and go indoors. I'm tempted to hide behind the door and hear your last words, but I make myself leave. I doubt those words would be very kind. I pad upstairs to the top of the house and reach my study, with its tall broad sills and its window box. The window is open. I lean out gently, careful to be quiet, and push the box slowly, across the sill. It glides like a dream. Down in the garden, you're still there, right where I left you, smoking in silence. If the window box fell, it might be me, or it might be an accident. People might guess, but no-one would know, there's only the wind and me up here. I know it's time.

I drop to my knees, hidden by the sill, and push the box as hard as I can, not thinking at all. I feel it slip, slide out of my touch, and then it's gone, just like Titanic on her final fall. I wait for the sound, a crash or a bang.

Instead, it's a thud, more of a clunk, like the sound you hear at a train station, when carriages join, connect together. I wait for more, the sound of a voice, the clatter of chairs. I hear, nothing.

Taking a breath, I go downstairs. It only takes seconds but it seems like hours from when I leave my lovely room to stepping outside, not sure what I'll see. You're there in the chair, still, silent. I don't look at Katie. You turn towards me.

'Nicely done,' you say, shortly.

It wasn't that hard, I think to myself. I don't bother saying, I've practised for ever.

You look at your watch, a little distracted. A trickle of blood runs under my feet.

'It's time I went and picked up the kids. Are you sure you're alright to sort out this mess?'

I nod, it's a yes, but you've already gone, round by the gate that leads to the street. I watch you go.

A thought flickers through my sad, little mind and refuses to leave, however I try. As I gather the courage to deal with Katie, with all of this blood, I see I've made a fatal mistake. I see I've chosen the wrong one.

Essential Purchase

Four short legs, covered in fur. No, not a dog, it was scattered with roses. Not my idea of a three-piece suite. And not from a shop, she bought it at the auction.

'Why spend all that money on crap?' I said to my girlfriend, Carolyn Price. Caro didn't answer, she didn't want to tell me, or maybe she thought her choice was clear. I just thought it was clearly awful, my squeaky-clean heart wanted so much better.

'I think we might have afforded a new one,' I told her, mildly, kicking it hard. The sofa rattled, I kicked it again. Sure enough, it made a noise.

'There's something inside,' I said surprised. Carolyn laughed.

'Coins,' she said. 'And more in the chairs, but I didn't have my cheque book, so I only bought this.' We grinned at each other across the chair. Now, I *thought* I understood.

I got out my penknife and leant across to slash the fabric. There was only one way to see inside.

'No!' shrieked Caro, grabbing my arm and then the knife. 'Leave it alone. I don't want it damaged.'

I shrugged, confused. And left it at that.

It turned out the sofa came with a history. It had once been installed in Carolyn's home, when she was still young, about thirteen, and just before her father died. Then they moved away, to another town, and the sofa, not wanted, was passed to a friend.

'I've been looking around for the suite forever,' Carolyn said as we sat on it later, drinking wine and reminiscing. 'I liked the chairs, but this is what counts. I spent most of my teenage years on here.' She smiled as she said this, patting the cushions and stroking the cloth and her eyes glittered with thoughts of the past. I liked the sofa a little bit less. I scowled, jealous, her words taking root as the sultry ghost of her teenage past sat beside me, lovely as ever. My heart beat fast.

'If you really insist on keeping this thing,' I said, grimly, 'you'll have to put it somewhere else. I won't have it here in the middle of the lounge. It's hideous, Caro. You can put it in the study, it'll just about fit.' The study, like my mind, was underused and overactive, full of clutter and last year's rubbish. I always thought I'd get around to sorting it out, but I never did, there was always something better to do. *Good riddance to you,* I said to the sofa. But I was wrong.

Caro was lovely but hard to love. She had long red hair and a temper to match, but, what was worse, bouts of depression which lasted for days. Carolyn didn't trust anyone fully, was always looking for someone to blame. She also needed lots of attention, it wore me out.

Once, she said she'd like to get married and I said, 'Fine, but maybe next year.' I think she knew I was putting her off. She wanted a ring to prove I meant it, something quite huge with bright coloured stones. I told her I couldn't afford a ring. That was a lie.

'You know my father killed himself,' she said to me then.

'Yes,' I affirmed, 'with a kitchen knife. But I know *you* won't.'

Her father's death had clearly hurt her, damaged her viewpoint, especially of men. But it hadn't damaged her love of knives, we had more of the things than a butcher's shop. And not all of them in the kitchen drawer.

Despite it all, I did love Caro, or I thought I did, and time went on. I couldn't commit to the wedding though. I kept her happy by buying her things.

A few weeks after the suite appeared, I met a new woman at work called Wilma. She was young and smart and dizzily blonde.

'What kind of a name is Wilma?' I said, regretting the words the moment I'd said them, but the woman just laughed.

'Mine,' she said, and gave me a look. 'You can buy me a coffee, for being so cruel.'

I bought her a coffee, and several more, it became a new habit I couldn't break. I loved being with Wilma, she was different from Caro, free and light-hearted, bubbly and fun. It wasn't that long before we were lovers.

My job involved a lot of travelling. Meeting my lover on jaunts out of town wasn't that hard. Lying to Carolyn wasn't hard either. I kept her amused with yet more stuff.

'You won't forget to get what I asked?' she'd said, one night, as she watched me pack. Her latest passion was Indian rugs. I'd promised to source at least a couple, but Wilma always helped me forget.

The house was becoming more and more full. I knew I'd have to do something soon.

'I think we've got enough furniture now,' I said mildly. 'And when I say that I also mean carpets.'

'But I want more,' said Carolyn, firmly, her eyes growing cold as she watched me cross to the car with things. Suits and shirts and casual clothes. Far too much for a working trip. She didn't comment.

I sighed heavily. I knew I should leave her, I just didn't dare. Carolyn angry was quite unstable, but Wilma increasingly wanted more. Wherever I looked, women wanted, sometimes I wished I was on my own. As I drove off, I swore, loudly. I'd knew I'd get Caro whatever she wanted, but whatever I bought, it wasn't enough. She tired of all the gifts and trinkets, except the sofa, and she bought that herself.

Months went by and nothing changed, except that Wilma grew more demanding.

'Let's go back to *your* place today,' she said, firmly.

'You know we can't, and you know why not,' I said, determined. But this time Wilma wouldn't give in. She was bored by now with our furtive lifestyle, wanted to make the 'us' official.

'But you told me Carolyn isn't there.'

'No,' I said, 'it wouldn't be right. It isn't my house, it's Caro's really.'

'So?' she said, dismissing my tender sensibilities, like she always did. She wore me down with her cool insistence, trampling over my good intentions. Not content with stealing the man, she wanted to have him in Caro's house.

'Fine,' I said, but I wasn't happy, and Wilma knew it but didn't care. Holding hands, we wandered around the empty house. Wilma was stunned, speechless almost.

'It's just like being in an antiques showroom,' she said, grinning. 'Classy, of course, but all the same... I never knew she had all this.' She stopped in front of an Indian rug. 'Now *that's* something,' she said, assessing. 'That has potential.'

'Just like you,' I agreed, laughing.

'But I'm not for sale,' said Wilma smoothly.

'Aren't you?' I asked, and pulled her towards me, kissing her once, then again and again. We stood on the hearthrug, glued together as her hand slid under my trouser belt. Her other hand deftly unbuttoned my shirt.

'No!' I said, as I reached for her zip, in between kisses. 'We can't, not here.'

'Well, where then lover?' said Wilma hotly, taking a break and nuzzling my neck. We edged upstairs, our arms round each other, eyes glazed over, with steamy lust. Down in the hall, the telephone rang. We both ignored it.

Reaching the top, we eased down the passage, heading for the bedroom, it still seemed wrong, but I didn't want to stop. We passed the study and the door was ajar, just a crack of light showing and Wilma stopped.

'What's in there?' she said, curious.

'Nothing,' I said, but I pushed the door with my foot, and it moved. We stared at the sofa.

'Perfect,' she said.

I had to agree. At least we wouldn't use Carolyn's bed. Except, the sofa was hers too. A family thing, a childhood memento. 'No,' I said, changing my mind, but lust was winning, and so was my lover. I knew the battle was already lost. The sofa blinked from behind the door.

'Darling don't argue,' Wilma insisted, dragging me firmly into the room. Light flooded in through the tiny window, showing up dust and years of tears. The faded old roses almost crackled, held in place by worn elastic. Wilma sat down and tested the springs; they squeaked noisily. Then I lowered myself onto the sofa, pressing Wilma into the cushions and enjoying that sense of something forbidden. Until she let out a terrible scream.

I leapt back up, she was clutching her hand and moaning softly, and something like blood was dripping down her wrist. It looked terrible. When I finally prised her fingers apart, I realised the cut wasn't that bad, I also saw what had caused the trouble. A knife was squeezed down the back of the sofa, crushed between the frame and the cushions. It looked pretty old, it was covered in rust. Or, it looked like rust.

'I think that knife's been there for years,' I said to Wilma, who was looking pale and rather cold. I threw it firmly onto the floor. Wilma said nothing. Her eyes were frozen and so ungiving.

'I think this knife could have been the one,' I started to say when I heard a noise, the slam of the door and Carolyn's footsteps on the stairs. Wilma and I glanced at each other. I know my face must have shown my fear. Carolyn, home, back from work, but far too early, she shouldn't be here. Her steps were measured, it was almost as if she expected us there. We sat, immobile, there wasn't time to escape from the room. The door opened and Carolyn's head appeared in the gap. She smiled slowly.

'Hello dearest,' she said to me. 'I thought you'd be here.'

Several thoughts rushed through my mind: that I should have answered the phone earlier, that the where of betrayal was worse than the deed. I moved my foot, revealing the knife. Caro came forward and stared at the thing.

'I wondered if I'd put it in there. That's why I wanted to buy the suite. It looks as if I was right, doesn't it?'

'Carolyn, darling, we should talk...' Light was starting to dawn, slowly, and bad as it was, the affair seemed safer. 'Why did you think I'd be here now?'

'Wilma told me, didn't you sweetie?' Carolyn turned and smiled at Wilma.

'What? Why?' I was confused. Why would Wilma do such a thing? I turned to my lover, apprehensive. 'I didn't even know you *knew* each other.'

'You silly man,' said Carolyn softly. Her look was warm and almost indulgent. 'Wilma and I are lovers, that's why.'

'But why on earth would you go with her?' I said, amazed, staring at Wilma and then at Caro. *I* was the one who was meant to be cheating. Carolyn grinned and in that moment I knew it all.

'She said she'd buy me a ring,' she said.

And then I see she's holding the knife.

Happy Ever After

They say the past comes back to haunt you and it's definitely true in my experience. The woman outside was banging on the door, thumping it loudly and making it shake. Making *me* shake, until I found out it was Marjorie Morris.

'I know you're in, Loreta Cavanagh. Open this door!'

Marjorie Morris was rather loud, but less of a threat than a three piece suite, so I opened the door. I knew she wouldn't take no for an answer. She slid in easily, which was quite an achievement given her size. I smiled weakly. She'd come about the event next Sunday, the party in the park. There was no escaping my contribution.

The rest of the morning passed quite pleasantly, discussing the stalls and the food arrangements. I'd lived in the street for several years, it was the perfect place for a single mum. Or, rather, it was, until Sal turned up.

By just after lunch, Marjorie Morris was ready to leave, so in theory I had the day to myself. I still dreaded a knock on the door. Since she'd returned to my life recently, I never knew when I'd next see Sal. As she left I watched Mrs Morris scanning the street just like me, but for different reasons. *She* was eyeing the latest stranger. He'd not lived here for very long, and I'd only seen him from behind, but I still knew he was too old for her.

'But not for you,' said Marjorie smiling. 'Perhaps he'll come to Sunday's picnic.'

'Along with his wife,' I said, mildly.

'And how would you know, unless you ask? Don't forget, you've run out of sugar.' Marjorie Morris walked away.

I shook my head, and scuttled inside. I wasn't taking any chances.

I first met Sally when we were twelve: she was slim and pretty with long fair hair. I wanted to look the same as her. Mum said no.

'Look at her eyes, they're cold and cruel. And her hair's so thin, you're fine as you are.'

I didn't agree, I knew I was dull, so I modelled myself on Sally's looks and copied her clothes. It didn't work. I was nothing like Sal in size or shape, we were chalk and cheese, from different worlds. We weren't even in the same class at school. Then boys appeared on my teenage radar and Sally vanished out of my life, until she turned up on a work placement. Time had passed, we were both at college, two different places, but both studying social care. We met on the train.

'Can I sit here?' Her voice was abrupt, the person beside me wasn't asking. I raised my eyes, ready to challenge, and saw Sally.

'Lori!' she said. 'I thought it was you.'

No you didn't, I thought, *but I saw you*. 'Was it you I saw at the centre last week? I thought it was but I wasn't sure.'

'It could have been me,' said Sal, grinning. 'I'm on placement there, from West Barn College. But let me guess, you're at the uni.' She said this with a touch of a sneer.

'But the course is the same,' I said, nodding, I was *so* pleased to see her. 'And the centre's the best, according to my tutor. A *huge* place and loads of experience.'

'You look different,' said Sally then, 'all grown-up.'

'I've a daughter now, she's just turned three. Her name's Emma.' This, proudly.

'And Mr Lori?' Sally asked.

'There isn't one,' I said bluntly. 'And that's how we like it.'

'Right,' said Sally, sounding doubtful. And that was that.

For the rest of the placement we worked together and studied together and spent all our time together, when we weren't working. I'd never had a friend like Sally before, a little bit scary, a little bit wild. It felt exciting. Part of me knew that Sally and I were *so* different, but I didn't mind that, it took me out of my comfort zone. After the too-short placement ended, we kept in touch, went out for drinks, despite our lives being worlds apart. It was great to have a mate of my own.

The day of the party in the park arrived, I'd just left the kids with one of the mums, when I felt the touch of a hand on my arm. I turned around and there was Sal. The wine in my hand went over the grass. I took a step back.

'I didn't expect to see you here,' I said, coldly. *Hoped you wouldn't be,* that's what I meant.

'That's hardly welcoming, Lori,' she said, looking amused. 'I wasn't aware the park was yours.'

'But the party is, it's for all the people who live round here. I don't remember giving you an invite.'

'I don't need you to give me an invite. I live here too.'

'You what?' I said. I couldn't believe it. I needed a drink to prop me up, but my wine had been spilt.

'With my husband, Lori, that little something you never managed to have and to hold.' The grip of her hand on my arm grew tighter and she twisted me round to look at the road. Someone was talking to Marjorie Morris. I knew who he was, the newcomer, the man she'd mentioned. I still couldn't see him all that well.

'*He's* your husband?' I said surprised, my words coming out as a kind of croak. My throat felt tight and I couldn't breathe.

'He certainly is,' said Sally, proudly. 'And quite a looker, in my opinion.' Her eyes narrowed, she hadn't forgotten. 'I'll be watching you, Lori Cavanagh. Just so you know.'

Sally liked people to be in her debt, she was able to make things happen that way, I'd seen the way she worked on others, somehow I thought she'd be different with me.

We were still on our courses and nearing the end. Passing the course was crucial to me, I needed to make a life for Emma. Passing the course could lead to a job. I'd only the final project to finish. Then my pc crashed and my work was gone.

'I don't believe you don't have a backup!' Sal said, incredulous, when I told her. She looked at me as if I was stupid. I was hysterical, almost distraught.

'I always meant to make a copy,' I said grimly. 'I just never got around to it, you know how it is. But I do have these.' I held up some notes. Notes was a rather ambitious word, what I actually had were three old books and a pile of scribbles.

'Everyone keeps a backup, Loreta,' Sally informed me. 'But at least your memory's still intact, the one in your brain. It is, isn't it?'

I looked at her coldly, this wasn't the time for sarcastic comments. Weeks of work had gone in an instant, I was gutted, stunned. 'The guy in the shop said the laptop's dead.'

'Great,' said Sal, 'but I've got an idea.' I waited, hopeful.

'I've got some notes, it's an essay really, it's on a similar topic to yours. I handed the thing in ages ago. You could use those notes if you'd think they'd help. At least they'd be something.'

'What, steal *your* work?' I said surprised, my first thought was *no*, but I couldn't help feel the lift of my heart. I needed to pass.

'It wouldn't be mine,' said Sal smoothly, 'it's not as if you'd copy the words. Just get the gist and borrow some quotes, add those to your tatty old notes. You'd write it out and make it yours. Just like reading a textbook, really.' She smiled lightly, she was *so* persuasive. And then she made her crucial point.

'It's not as if we're at the same college. No-one would know, no-one at all.'

That was the moment to walk away, to laugh it off, to go to the tutor and tell the truth, or maybe say I was ill or something. I could have done a number of things. Of course, I didn't do any of those. They were far too risky.

'Ok, Sal, I'll borrow your work, but only as hints, and nothing else.' We both knew it was more than that. 'Thanks, Sal, I'm really grateful.'

'Not a problem, kid,' she said. But it was, a big one.

Later that day and all through the night I worked on the project, and thanks to Sal and an endless stream of strong coffee I finished in time. The work was better than my last attempt which didn't help my guilty conscience. I now owed Sally my whole future. I never forgot it.

Not that it stopped me stealing her boyfriend.

My course had finished and so had Sally's, but we kept in touch, like we had before. Her results came in ahead of mine, and she'd done really well, *and* got a job, while I was still looking. I didn't mind, I was still so grateful I'd made it through. Glad to share in Sally's success. And then I met Rob.

It all began on New Year's eve, we were off to a party and Sally was bringing the boyfriend along. For once in her life she was really keen, which was not like her. They'd even talked of getting engaged.

'It's time you gave me *your* opinion.'

'It's far too soon, that's my opinion.'

'Just wait 'til you meet him. He's ever so cool.'

'I don't care,' I warned Sally. 'It's still too soon.'

Sally just shrugged.

Soon after ten, they both turned up, they'd been drinking a lot, but that was ok, it was New Year's eve. Sally was dressed in shimmering white. She shoved her bloke in front of my face. 'Lori, meet Rob.'

I opened my mouth to say hello, but words didn't come. I'd read all about those heart-stopping moments, the ones that happen in magazines, where you meet a new bloke and the world stands still, but that had never happened to me, never, not once. Until that night, when he leant towards me, and kissed me hard. Fireworks fizzed and champagne corks popped but it wasn't even midnight, the magic, the buzz was all in my head. I looked at Rob after we stopped and I think we both knew something had happened. It was a flash in the pan, it didn't last long, but it did mean the end of my friendship with Sal. She never forgave me for stealing her bloke.

'We were going to make the announcement that night! And to think I helped you pass your course, gave you the paper, that got you through. Remember, Lori?'

Of course, I remembered, I'd never forget. I still felt guilty months later. But I never thought she'd do anything about it.

When my passion with Rob died down, I tried to win back Sal's friendship, but it didn't work so I moved away and that was the last I saw of Sally. Until she turned up on the street one day, a few days before the party in the park. It wasn't the warmest reunion ever.

'You want to be careful Lori Cavanagh. I'll tell that place where you work the truth. That the paper you wrote was 'borrowed' from me. And where will your job be then, I wonder? Your qualifications all mean nothing.' Her eyes narrowed and she leaned in close, all the better to smell my fear. 'I'd do it now, if not for your kids. I won't take food from the mouths of babes. But years from now, things will have changed. So, take note, keep away from my husband.'

'But I don't even know who your husband is,' I said, wildly. My heart was pounding. Sally just laughed and walked away.

After that day, I saw her everywhere, at the shops, on our street and even by the school, although as far as I knew she didn't have any kids. She was always at a distance, never up close, but I knew it was her, and I tried to keep my distance too. I was so scared she'd tell everyone.

Then, a few weeks later, before the party, we passed in the street, and I made her stop, I was tired of all the sleepless nights, of wondering how I'd get a new job, if it all came out. I couldn't go down without a fight.

'You were the one who gave me the paper. You'd be telling on yourself, as well as me.'

'There's no proof I was ever involved, it's only your word, and that doesn't count. My course was finished by then. And unlike you, I don't need a job. And there's more. But you'll have to wait.'

'You can't do that,' I said, desperate, wanting to know the worst that could happen, but Sally had already turned away, almost ran and rounded the corner. I stared after her. I never knew when I'd see her again.

When I did, she dropped her bombshell.

'It wasn't my work I gave you, Lori, that was a lie. It was Lou Abercrombie's, I'd promised I'd get it back from her tutor. A lucky break, but not for Louise.' Her face hardened.

'You'll never prove I helped you do it. Not that you'd want to prove it, would you? But *I* might want to drop some hints, tell a few people what I know. I'll never forgive you for stealing Rob.'

'You gave me the paper before I met him. I thought you wanted to help me pass.'

'I wanted to have something on you, and I had the chance, so I took that chance. You never know when such knowledge might be useful. I didn't know then I'd have to use it.' She grinned disarmingly. 'Besides, I never liked Abercrombie. That you both needed my help was lucky.'

I still didn't get the point of it all. 'But years have gone by, why threaten me now?'

'I'm not threatening you, this little chat is in lieu of a warning. To keep you away from someone who's mine. Like I should have done then, when you first met Rob.' She frowned, thinking. 'I'm also annoyed about something else, something you should have told me about. Shouldn't you Lori?'

I could feel my anxiety levels rising. 'You'll have to excuse me Sally,' I said. 'I'm due at the school in thirty minutes.'

Her last little comment had freaked me out. Whatever she knew, or thought she knew, she couldn't be sure, nobody could, apart from me. But I knew she wouldn't leave me alone, would always be there, in the street, watching. I'd have to move.

My heart sank. I didn't want to move away, this was my home, my children's home, but I couldn't risk my whole career, my children's future, just for that. *And* I felt guilty, thinking about my son and his father. Neither knew the other existed. It was one more betrayal, one more thing that shouldn't have happened, but Sally couldn't *know*, Rob didn't know, and neither did my mother, so how could she?

I chewed on my lip. I couldn't let Sally ruin my life, or chase me out of the place I loved. I thought I might give it one last try, beard the lion in her den, knock on her door and beg for a truce. I stumbled down the road blindly, legs like lead.

I'd never met Sally's wonderful husband, the closest I'd come was seeing him talking to Marjorie Morris. But I had this feeling I'd know his face. And I was right.

The door opened, he looked quite different, it wasn't surprising, time had passed and I'd never seen him this close up. Not recently. He'd gained some weight and a pair of glasses and lost some hair. But he still looked good and just like my son.

'Hello Rob,' I said, weakly.

'Lori!' he said. 'So it's really you.' He smiled warmly. 'When Marjorie Morris mentioned your name, I didn't know you were *that* Loreta, although I have to admit, I did wonder. She only said you were pretty and single.' His eyes twinkled. 'Do come in.'

So Sally never mentioned my name, I thought. She must have been worried and so was I. How could I keep my son away now, but if I didn't what would happen? I wondered if it could get any worse. The time for kindness and charm was over.

'Is Sally in?' I said bluntly. 'I'm sorry Rob, but I have to see her, now if possible.'

His eyes darkened. 'Sally?' he said. He didn't move.

'Your wife,' I affirmed, feeling impatient. 'I've something I need to say to you both, now if I could. You need to hear it. Is she in?'

Rob didn't answer, just turned around and walked down the passage, into the lounge. I followed him in. I found him leaning against the table.

'She's dead, Loreta,' he said, hoarsely. 'She died last year, in that storm we had, the one where all the trees came down. I can't believe that nobody said, but of course I didn't live here then.' He sounded faint, absent-minded. 'And then of course, you'd fallen out. Because of me.' His voice trailed off.

I wanted to say it wasn't his fault, but I opened my mouth and the words wouldn't come. I tried again, but no, nothing. I wanted to say, *she can't be dead, I saw her only the other day.* I watched a woman pass by the window, she was slim and pretty with long fair hair. I can hear her voice in my head now, can feel the touch of her hand on my arm.

'You'll never be free of me,' she said.

The Last Bus Home

Of all the possible forms of travel, I like the train. Taking the train makes me feel like a queen, that long, smooth ride, the velveteen chairs and the buffet bar with its cellophane cakes and cups of tea. I love it all.

I even like walking the length of the carriage. Don't underestimate walking about: it's fine to *imagine* striding along, but actually treading those carpet tiles, that's a whole different story

But despite my love of life on the rails, one summer's day, I caught the bus. It wasn't my choice, I was stuck in Pornath, miles from home, and wanted to get back to Califron Fields, which is where I live. It's a lovely place but out in the sticks.

'You should be taking the car,' said Roy.

Roy was my bloke, we lived together in a tiny house, and we'd had this argument over and over. He knew the reason I wouldn't drive. Two simple words: Califron Hill. The place was notorious.

A long, steep slope, just out of Sheritin (this was Google). *Watch for the bends, they go on and on. An*

uneven camber and vicious twists. Then came the comments.

'A scorcher of a ride, my best one ever!'

'How many cars can I overtake?'

'That final bend: I could do it faster!'

And, sadly, they did. The Hill itself had a number of bends on its upward slope, steep and steeper, approaching the top with a killer of a turn, first to the left, then to the right, both of which made my stomach curl, made me feel the world had been twisted, was spinning and turning itself upside down. And me with it. Which is just what happened.

Roy, of course, being a man, and robust, thought my fears were all in my head. He loved to go fast.

'I'm telling you Helen,' he said stoutly, 'this car might be small but she glides up the slope.' He patted the bonnet of his brand new sports car, glossy and green, and I had to agree. It had three times the power of my old Fiesta, but I'd tried the Hill in a car before, and twice before that: never again. The solution was simple, I went on the train.

Only on that day the train wasn't running.

'Maintenance on the Califron Line,' said a bright yellow notice, almost a smile, as it stood right by the station entrance. 'Alternative transport will be provided.' For which, read a bus.

I had to go. Siân, my sister was getting married and today was meant to be dress-fitting day. My neighbour would take me, it was fine going down, downhill slopes were as easy as pie. It was coming back up that I found so difficult. Time for the bus.

'Can't see the difference, myself,' said Roy. 'A car or a bus, it's all much the same.' But Roy was wrong.

A bus was bigger, far more powerful. And more to the point, I'd be higher up, so the bends wouldn't make me feel so rough, the road wouldn't seem at such an angle, and neither would I.

Roy grunted, he didn't understand. He loved his car and he liked to drive fast, going up a hill was sport to him. I liked his car too, when it kept to the flat.

If I'm being honest, was it all my fault? If I'd have been braver and gone in his car it wouldn't have happened. If I'd not needed change and talked to the driver, the coach might have been a bit further along. If I hadn't seen Roy, amazed he was there, overtaking the bus in his neat little sports car, and stood up and waved, things might have been different. If, if, if.

But all those ifs are a waste of time, what happened, happened and it's too late now to change the result. The car overtaking, cutting in front, Roy at the wheel and the urgent squeal of the brakes of the bus. The twist and the turn on an ugly bend as the driver managed to miss the car. The scream in my head and the words on my lips and the dark red blood, dripping on the road. The deadly. Silence.

Now it's all over I have to ask. Was my fear of Califron Hill, less about fear and more in the way of a premonition?

Twelve Months On

My name's Siân, I'm Helen's sister, I was the one whose wedding it was. Emphasis, *was*. Do I feel guilty? Of course I do. I was the reason she was on that bus. I'll think of that accident all of my life, of Roy's green car which was going too fast, I know it was, my sister's boyfriend, terrible wreckage, wrecked remains and the end of a life. Over and over and over again. Stop.

I cancelled the wedding, there wasn't much choice and it turned out to be a permanent arrangement. Rick, my fiancé, didn't seem bothered and he soon found himself a life in Bali. I gather the expat girls are gorgeous. Bali was where we were going for our honeymoon. I don't expect I'll go there now.

Some months after that terrible day, which killed my sister, I finally tired of being so sad. I was all cried out, and a strange sort of calm had possessed my soul. Rick was gone and so was Helen, the only ones left were Roy and me and a cat called Fliss. I first met Fliss at the rescue home, we took to each other, and she tells me things, she jumps on my knee when Roy's coming home, and sharpens her claws like mad on my legs. She knows *everything*.

After what happened, Roy and I were always together, talking and grieving, wondering if we'd made it happen, me with my dress and him with his car and then, at last, when Rick walked out, it seemed only right for Roy to move in. The police didn't think he'd caused the crash, they talked a lot about bends and camber. We were all stunned that a man in an open top car could survive while a girl in a bus was crushed and killed. 'Perhaps it was meant,' said Roy, once. I didn't answer.

My family, of course, weren't very happy when Roy moved in, especially Mum.

'But Siân, lovey, it's thanks to that man that Helen died. And Rick left.'

'It's not as if we're a couple, Mum.' But that little comment passed her by.

My Dad didn't even try to persuade me. He simply said that Roy wasn't welcome in his house, and that meant I wasn't welcome either, unless I came on my own, in secret. I didn't want to do that. I felt at the time, it was important to be loyal. To someone anyway.

The door opens and Roy comes in, back from his job at the market garden. I can't remember when it happened, when Roy moved out of the small spare room and shifted his body into my bed. I thought it would make things easier somehow, make him trust me, make him feel calm. I remembered Roy from before the crash, daredevil, crazy, wild about driving. He changed after, became sadder, morose, a little bit wiser, although not so much he doesn't drive.

After we've eaten, he goes upstairs, he spends night after night alone in the bedroom, playing games on his new pc. I think he feels the games are safer. Fliss and I just sit by the fire, dreaming and waiting, Fliss, of mice and an ice-cold day when the fire's on, and me, just waiting, always waiting. I don't like to think about why I'm waiting.

After the crash, it was Dad who asked me the crucial question. 'Why was Roy on the road anyway? Helen must have thought she'd left him at home.' And it's true, she did, she told me so, when we had our lunch, just after the fitting. I remember that lunch, I had lasagne while she had salad and we laughed and said we should have swapped, I was the one who was getting married. But I was also the thinner girl. So, when Dad asked me where Roy had been, I couldn't think of a suitable answer. They knew he wouldn't be driving to fetch her, knew how she felt about Califron Hill. So I just said nothing, and Mum, I guess, was simply puzzled, but I saw from Dad's face, he'd guessed the truth.

Roy and I had been seeing each other. Before the crash, before she died.

'Such a daredevil thing to do,' I'd said, then wished the words erased straight away. I'd meant his trip to visit me, not the route he took, or the way he drove, but Roy didn't seem to understand. He blamed himself. I wondered, did I?

Time passed, and I missed my sister, more than I realised, I wanted her back. But she wasn't coming back, not now, not ever and the worms of doubt crept into my mind. What had we done, Roy and I, and what could I do to make things right? The answer was nothing.

Ellie Stevenson

Fliss looks up. She's heard a noise, something like mice, the slightest creak, the floorboards shifting but there aren't any mice and there never have been, Fliss is too good a mouser for that. But something's there and I know it's time, the waiting is over.

I make my way to the door slowly. It's almost a year since Helen died, and the weather is lovely, hazy and warm, the perfect evening. Careful to be quiet, I open the door, which creaks slightly, despite the oil I smear on the hinges every few days. I stop and listen, I can't hear Roy, who's still upstairs so I open the door a little bit wider and beckon slowly. Fliss gets up and stretches and yawns, a twitch of her whiskers shows she approves. Fliss can see what most of us can't, including, my sister.

I beckon again. 'It's okay Helen,' I say softly, 'it's safe to come in, Roy's upstairs, the first on the left. You know where to go.' Along with her man, I'd taken her house, but she doesn't seem to mind.

I retreat to the lounge, picking up Fliss and walking slowly, we're both keeping our ears peeled, waiting to see what Helen will do. We're both waiting to hear a noise, both waiting to hear him yell. I smile at Fliss.

At last, I know where my loyalties lie.

Under the Tree

It's a cold night, when there aren't any stars in the sky anymore, when the sky is just black. When night becomes day and the sun's just a hollow ball in the sky. Empty, without light.

When the straps on your bra are all the better to hang you with.

As if I could, and if I could, could reach that high, tell me Mother, why would I bother?

Perhaps for leaving me dead in the park, buried within my tomb by the fountain, where even the dogs don't drink anymore. Where the children always cry for their nannies. I wonder what having a nanny is like?

I didn't have a nanny, or even a nurse, I only had you, and *you* were useless, you only wanted to shut me up, make me be quiet, so you could smoke and shag your man, lying beneath the old oak tree. I bet you didn't know I knew about that, that you weren't just hugging or lying there. I bet you thought I was far too young. But I wasn't too young to die, was I?

I wasn't too young to be missed either, although not by you.

The trees missed me with their huge-petalled-leaves and the fruit that bounced on the ground below. Tiny acorns growing so tall, the promise of life. Ha! to that.

The wind missed me, me and my scarf, missed blowing it all around my head and wrapping it round my throat like a vice.

The sky missed me, like I missed my kite when it drifted away, up to heaven, never to return.

But you didn't miss me, not one little bit, even in that place they sent you to, the one with the bars.

If I was alive I wouldn't be here, waiting for you to come back, at last.

But, in the end, somebody came.

The man, your shag, the one who gave you a ring at last, he hasn't changed, he still looks shifty, even now, even after all these years have passed. He looks nervous, keeps looking around and tapping his fingers on an empty packet of cigarettes. There's a kid with him, a little boy, he reminds me of someone, I can't think who. Then there's the woman.

The woman's in charge and she looks rather grim and doesn't speak much. She walks to the fountain and glares at the statue, scowls at the stone. It's green and covered in mildew now, graffiti too. It won't be missed and nor will the fountain. All things come to an end in time. Except my wait. But here they come.

Men in their suits, all bagged up. Diggers and workers, faceless and bleak, ready to go to work on the soil. But you're not here, why aren't you here, looking just the same, in your short wool coat and your tight pink skirt, pretending you're thirty or twenty, or less? Instead of being older, forty or more. I bet you don't remember *where*. But somebody does, that's why they're here. And not before time.

It's boring, waiting, the digging goes on, and on, and on. Still you don't come. The weather gets warmer, the men start to sweat and the hole gets deeper and wider too. The woman frowns.

'There's nothing here,' says one of the men, a policeman I think, shaking his head, as he looks at his boss and the woman seems angry. She swears at your bloke, and wimp that he is, he backs away, into the boy. Your shag doesn't notice.

'Try over there,' says the woman sharply, pointing an elegant, painted finger. And then they find it.

'Guv, over here!' The coppers come running, and a sudden sharp sadness crosses her face. It's gone in an instant like mist in the early part of the day. I tell myself I know what they'll find.

'It's the boy,' says a voice, and the man starts to cry, wimpering really, your hubby, I mean. He's so pathetic. And who's this boy and why is he there? What about me?

I glance at your bloke, he lies on the ground, sobbing, useless. 'Forgive me,' he says and I think he means you, but I'm not really sure. I look for the child but the boy is gone. And then I know.

I never guessed you'd hidden the other.

Such a long time in jail, such a very long time, fifteen years. I suppose it's fair, for killing a child. That's what they told me, over and over. I suppose it's true.

But even they had to let me out.

The first thing I did was go to the fountain and put down some flowers.

They rebuilt it after, it's a public park and it looks just the same, even to me. There's a grave of course, for my little boy, with a proper black headstone, but they won't let me go there, it's part of the terms. I think that's cruel, but I understand. So I put my flowers on the fountain instead.

There's nobody else to do that now.

My husband left me after the sentence, he helped me confess, then buggered off. It was too much to take, he didn't want to face it. They said he broke down and cried at the scene, I don't see why. It wasn't even his son who had died. I think he thought the kid was his, but not a chance. And still they didn't find the girl.

I never told them where she was.

They'll never find my daughter now, not after all this time has passed. She's not far away, just up the shelter, the place seemed apt, she often used to wait for me there. The tree's close by, I know that tree well, and the roots were a pain and hard to avoid.

Nobody even missed the girl, despite her being older, no-one at all, not even me.

I only missed my little boy, no more than a baby, the light she destroyed when she picked up that pillow and held it firmly over his face. She snuffed out his life in just a few seconds. I asked her once why she did such a thing, even shook her to make her say, but she never said why, I don't think she knew. I didn't even try to forgive her. I never told, for years and years, until I confessed, to something, *she'd* done. So the boy I'd carried could be laid to rest. But as for her…

I'm sure *you* think I meant to kill her. But it isn't true, I covered it up, my little boy's death, but the wound festered and I just lashed out, once too often, and there she was, dead on the floor. I didn't care, how could I care, after all that had happened? I only asked her to mind him once. Or maybe a few times, I can't recall. Burying my boy nearly broke my heart, but I did it for her, thinking it right. She was only a child at the time, after all. But it wasn't right, it could never be right, although it gave me some needed practice, for when I had to do it again. Such a terrible thing.

I was bored in prison and fifteen years takes a long time to live, and I'd never had any life before, this was my chance to make things different. I discovered I had a gift for stories, odd sort of stories, mad and macabre or maybe that's just the person I was. Everybody loved the stories I wrote. They didn't love me.

My prison tutor was thrilled to bits, he said my work was really authentic. Well, it would be, wouldn't it?

My daughter, you see, she needed to tell, to make things better. And she couldn't, could she, being dead and gone, and under the tree. So I did it for her, I told her story, to set things straight, even though I said it was me, not her.

Of course, it's only a story, right? My tutor said, to make it *real*. The boy was real, but only the boy, and that was an accident.

Go to the park and look at the tree, it gets bigger and bigger each year that passes. The roots are a pain, they've taken over, no-one could lie and have sex there now. That tree won't be moved and nor will the roots. Even the police would be challenged to find her.

But that's ok, it's only a story, there is no girl.

You hope.

Watching Charlotte Brontë Die

We'd been in the flat a year when it happened.

The night had been cold, and extremely wet. I was sitting in my chair, over by the window.

My wife was out working, she usually was. It was then that I heard it, an enormous crash, a screech and a thud, followed by silence. Someone's life, played out on the pavement. It wasn't the first time our street had done that, claimed a victim, with its deadly camber, its rain-stroked curve. The road was treacherous, sometimes lethal.

I leapt from my chair and ran to the window. She was lying there, in the middle of the tarmac, broken, damaged, her head to one side. She was calm and quiet and didn't move, and the bike beside her was bent out of shape. My heart stopped beating. It was Charlotte Brontë.

And it looked to me as if she was dead.

I dressed quickly, with trembling fingers, opened the door and ran down the stairs. The street would be empty, it was access only, apart from the tourists. There were no tourists on the street that night. I opened the door that led to outside and looked to the right, she'd be just around the bend. I rounded it quickly, as fast as I could. There was nobody there.

I blinked sharply and looked again, in case I'd missed her. I saw the rain, it was heavier now, streaming down gutters, flooding the road. I saw the light on an empty can, a broken bottle, remains of a toy. But that was all. No bike wheels spinning high in the air, no ghastly corpse, or crumpled victim propped against a wall. The street was damp and devoid of life, but also of death. I watched the water running away. All I could think was one small thought. I hadn't known Charlotte could ride a bike.

It wasn't the first time I'd seen her.

My wife has a job at the local uni, teaching English, she loves all things Brontë. That's how we met, at a Brontë conference, in West Yorkshire. I married my wife because I love her, but also because she looks like Charlotte. I should feel guilty, but I don't, not at all. I'm privately pleased and secretly proud, as if I've discovered a hidden treasure. Perhaps I have.

Charlotte Brontë, born again.

My skills and training are different from my wife's. *I'm* not a teacher, I'm a writer's researcher, but that's ok, I love my work. I study theology as well as the Brontës, ferret out the facts from the archives. And I love the place where I find those facts, a cathedral library, and that's the place where I first saw Charlotte. Not in one of the first editions, but there in person, right by the shelves.

I was up in the gallery, quietly working. Dozens of volumes piled up high. They were all so beautiful, all so original, it's a wonder I did any work at all. I was taking a tract from the nearest shelf when I heard a noise and looked right down to the room below and there she was, right beneath me, and all lit up from the stained glass windows. I caught my breath. She was just like the photos, quaint and homely with a small, shy smile and rosebud lips. But her eyes were different, cool, piercing and quite unlike the rest of her look. Even though we were far apart, and I was standing up in the gallery, I could see those eyes, see them stare through me. I watched and waited, noticed her beckon. But she still didn't speak.

Forgetting where I was, I walked over to the railing. I forgot that the railing, normally solid and made of cast iron, had been replaced by a tape for repairs. Nobody ever came up here. All there was between me and a fall, a terrible drop, maybe death, was a thin strip of tape, not even taut. I was seconds away from the worst that could happen. I stopped suddenly, looked down at the floor. Miss Brontë had gone. I was safe, for the moment.

But she always came back.

A few weeks later, I was in the library, just for a change. The rain poured down on an autumn day. It was normally dark, the building was old, but today felt different, colder somehow. I shivered in the chill, caught in the alcove by the spiral staircase. The room I was in was called the Cage, it was small and narrow with a strange metal door, more like a gate. Somewhat reminiscent of an old-fashioned lift in a French hotel. I was looking for a book but couldn't find it, was thinking I'd have to go upstairs and visit the gallery once again. I wasn't keen. I peered up the staircase and there was Charlotte, sitting at the top.

Her dark brown dress looked very real and so did she, she was reading a book. I wanted to touch her, stretch out a hand, but I thought if I did, she'd vanish like mist. So I smiled instead.

She ignored me completely.

Unable to resist, I walked towards her, and as I moved closer, the book she was reading slid out of her hands and fell to the floor. A cloud of dust filled my vision. When I could see, Miss Brontë had gone. I picked up the book.

It wasn't like any I'd seen before.

It was bound in tissue, a filigree pattern in black and gold. It was written in verse, an ode to a friend who was clearly dead. The author's name was Charlotte Brontë. I paused, thinking. A little more checking told me the book was a limited edition, it was bound to be priceless. I doubted the library knew they had it. I sat there for ages, admiring the cover, smoothing the binding and lost in thought.

I thought of the library, it was beautiful but old and needed money, a lot of money. This book could fund it.

I thought of my wife, her passion, her research into all things Brontë. This book could fuel it.

I thought of myself, how much I wanted *anything* at all of hers I could get. This book was it.

I stroked the cover and sated my eyes on my Brontë find. Then I bundled it into my scruffy old bag and took it home. That book was my downfall.

I was plagued with guilt so, at first, I did nothing, I simply hid it under the mattress. Then my wife complained of a lumpy bed, so next I moved it into the oven: my wife never cooks. But when she talked of guests coming round, for the first time ever, I moved it again, to a shabby old suitcase that lived in the hall. It went in the lining, right at the bottom. There it stayed until I saw her, dead, in the street.

There was no-one there.

When I returned from the dripping wet night, I took out the book, and read it all, from cover to cover. It didn't take long. What I read was something of a shock. It was an ode to a friend who had died, yes. But the name of the friend was Howard Cole. My name! Then I fell ill.

It started off as a simple virus, a nasty bug, dementia and sweat. And terrible pain, just like the sort you'd get from a fall. But I'd had no fall, I'd stopped in time, seconds before I went over the edge. Or so I thought.

My wife, Cameron, was ever so patient, she cancelled her teaching and offered to take me abroad for a while, but I refused. I wanted to be here, in the heart of Yorkshire, next to Haworth, next to Charlotte. Not that I said so.

Time passed but the pain didn't, it went up my spine and into my heart, stopped me from walking or leaving our flat. It kept me inside, bound to a chair with wheels and support. Sometimes, on good days, I could walk with a cane but never for long. And worst of all, I couldn't go back to my work or the library, go and see Charlotte by the shelves. Instead, I'd the time to dwell on my thoughts, dwell on my guilt for stealing the book. But I didn't give it back.

'The doctor thinks that you'll soon get better,' my wife insisted, after a week, then two, then three. I hoped she was right. But the weeks went by, then months, then a year, and I just sat there, trapped in my chair and unable to move. All I could do was glide around, from polished room to polished room, while the tests went on and nobody knew what the problem was. I sat watching the tourists pass, peering out of our bedroom window. My wife had long since gone back to work.

'Students to see, places to go,' she'd said, rather cruelly.

Then it was Spring. I was sitting in the chair, round about lunchtime, when my wife came home. I heard her moving about in the hall, dragging a suitcase out from the cupboard. I heard her filling it up with things, dashing between the hall and the bedroom. She sounded to be in some sort of rush. I followed her footsteps into the bedroom, studied her movements, watched her work. Folding her clothes and filling up space. At last she sat back and paused for breath.

'Are you going on some sort of trip?'

Cameron blinked, the way she did when fazed or unsure.

'Why, Howard, I'm leaving you,' she said, slowly.

I nodded, agreeing, I couldn't pretend I hadn't guessed. 'It's alright, I understand. You don't want to live with a man in a wheelchair. I don't blame you.' But inside I felt my heart thumping. My wife looked surprised.

'You think I'd leave you because you've been ill? Oh no, Howard, it's not about that. It's because of that woman, Charlotte Brontë. I can't stand the way you are about her. Howard, she's dead!'

I must have looked stunned.

'How could you think I didn't know?' Cameron said. Her full name was Cameron Charlotte, it was one more thing they had in common. She closed the case on the bed with a snap.

'I'm leaving now,' she said, firmly. 'I've arranged for a nurse and a cook to call.'

'Don't bother,' I said, shortly. 'I can manage alright, I don't need their help.'

'Oh I think you do,' she said, pensive, 'I think you do.'

I waited until she'd left the flat, walked down the stairs and closed the front door. I listened and heard her steps fading, the high pitched clip on the uneven street. Then I pushed on the arms of the chair firmly and tried to stand up. It was very hard, but I managed to do it.

I struggled slowly into the hall with the help of the cane. I was looking for the suitcase, the one with the book, but the case had vanished, along with its contents. We had three suitcases all the same, it was just my luck she'd taken the largest. Or was it luck?

I returned to the bedroom, slowly, thinking, wondering how I'd get the book back and knowing I wouldn't. I staggered to the window, guessing my wife would have long since gone, but having to look. I was tired and weary, in so much pain. It seemed to take hours, a lifetime almost. I leant against the glass which had misted over, feeling exhausted, my wife had gone, and with her, my treasure. My life was over.

I rubbed on the pane, and tried to see out, it was bright and sunny, a beautiful day, for everyone else. My eyes widened. There, in the street, stood Charlotte Brontë, and she wasn't dead, she was standing, upright, and looking at me. It could, perhaps, have been a trick of the light.

But then, she winked.

AUTHOR'S NOTES

These stories are fiction, but a few aspects are based on fact. The cathedral library in the title story is based on York Minster Library, an amazing building with some lovely books and architectural features. Visit it if you can. I also recommend the works of Charlotte Brontë and her sisters, and a visit to their parsonage in Howarth, Yorkshire. The island in *Anna Grail* is based on Sark, in the Channel Islands, a beautiful place. The characters in this story are in no way connected to anyone on the island.

York Minster: www.yorkminster.org

Brontë Society: www.bronte.org.uk

Sark Tourism: www.sark.co.uk

ACKNOWLEDGEMENTS

Thanks to James Allwright for another wonderful cover design which was suitably atmospheric and to Jann Tracy for her support and encouragement. It makes all the difference. Thank you both.

ABOUT THE AUTHOR

Ellie Stevenson is a freelance writer, who writes on history, careers, travel and the arts. She has lived in one of the largest and one of the smallest islands in the world.

Website: www.elliestevenson.co.uk

Blog: http://elliestevenson.wordpress.com

Twitter: http://twitter.com/Stevensonauthor

Facebook:
http://www.facebook.com/Stevensonauthor

OTHER WORKS BY THE AUTHOR

Ship of Haunts: the other Titanic story (novel). Extract follows.

Extract from Ship of Haunts

1
Carrin's Story – 2012

Not every girl gets stalked by a ghost. Or haunted by a ship.

The ghost was called Lily but the ship came first. It always did. The ship was Titanic. I drowned on that ship.

I was up on the deck, right at the top, running and running, as fast as I could, towards the stern. Away from the water, around my feet. I wasn't alone.

And though I ran fast, as fast as I could, the stern rose up, out of the water, and we rose with it, slipping and sliding on a frigid deck. Not everyone made it.

I grabbed for a railing and held on tight, feeling the steel dig into my skin. I knew it was hopeless. Loads of others did just the same. And then the stern shifted, twisted and turned, a corkscrew ride, high in the air. We held our place, just for a second. Then down she fell, faster and faster, heading for the bottom, where no-one goes. And then I fell off.

My arms flailed and I let out a scream, one more voice, in amongst the rest.

'I'm going to die. I'm going to die.'

And die is exactly what I did.

But unlike the others, I had help.

I said there was a ghost and her name was Lily. Not that I knew she was called Lily to begin with, she was just a voice, driving me crazy. I first met Lily in 1912, when I lived before. Now you know it. I *am* crazy.

Well maybe you're right, but why don't you ask me where we met?

We met on Titanic, which sank in the night on her maiden voyage, in 1912.

Such a beautiful ship, sailing the ocean, and then – nothing.

So many died – fifteen hundred people, it was tragedy, failure, on dozens of counts.

And the last sentence, very important.

I was there.

2
Lily's Story – 1911

I was proud to be called a Yorkshire girl, Yorkshire had made me what I was. I never wanted to leave the north. But since I had…

When Mother gave me the crumpled letter I knew it was bad. Give it to Maddy, is what she said. Maddy will help. I didn't care. I knew it was bad, without the letter, her white, pinched face and the constant cough. I opened the letter. Just as I thought.

Lucie and I had to go south. To a place called Southampton.

Three days later, my sister emerged from Mother's bedroom. Her face was pale, pale as a ghost. 'Mother's gone,' she said to me sadly. 'What will we do?'

I pulled the letter out of my pocket. 'We're off to Southampton, to stay with our aunt, Madeleine Rawlins. Mother arranged it.' Lucie blinked.

Lucie was distant, dark and plump, not a bit like me. I was tall and fair, with thin skinny bones and flyaway hair. Lucie was pretty, I had to protect her.

I thought Southampton would keep us safe, keep the wolf from the door. How wrong can you be?

Aunt Maddy's house was a total shock. We'd lived in a farmhouse, out in the fields, in a place called Linsit. Linsit was vast, with moors and the cliffs, and the Bay below, with us in between. We were renting a farm and managing somehow, until Mother died. Aunt Maddy's house was right in the town, it was tall and thin, just like her. She didn't seem all that pleased to see us.

'So you're Lucie?' she said to my sister, her cold eyes sharp. Lucie just stood there, silent, as always. Maddy was dark, like Lucie was dark, but Madeleine Rawlins' face was cold. She was watchful and wary and didn't look like my mother at all. I didn't warm to this woman one bit. But I had to try.

'Good to meet you at last, Aunt Maddy,' I said to her, firmly, taking her hand. She didn't bother to look my way.

'I'm not your aunt,' she insisted sharply, looking at Lucie. 'I'm far too young to be anyone's aunt.' It was true she was, being barely thirty, and now expecting a child of her own. But she *was* my aunt, my mother's sister. I also thought she was Lucie's aunt. My mistake.

Her man, Joss Rawlins, who she called her husband, had just got a job. He was a stoker by trade, he worked on the ships, shovelling coal. Or at least, he had, until the strike started. No-one had worked on the ships in months, because of the coal strike. For a place like Southampton, which lived by its docks, the strike was bad news. And it made Joss restless, hungry for change.

I knew how he felt, I was restless too, I wanted a life, a world full of colour, not grey, grimy streets and second-hand clothes. I had my adventures, stealing mostly, we needed the food. I loved the excitement. I also stole things I could pawn later.

But a new dawn was coming, a ship called Titanic, and Joss signed up. I could see it in his eyes, he was eager to leave. To be fair to the bloke, it can't have been easy, his woman expecting and two teenage girls who weren't his own. It was then I had my fatal idea.

I thought it would give us, Lucie and me, a much better future. I also thought it would free up Mad.

That was my third and final mistake.

3
Carrin's Story – 1995

When I was nine, I began to remember. We lived in Linsit, in a house by the sea. We were up on the cliffs, as high as a kite. It felt like that, the wind was so strong it blew you along. Sometimes it almost blew you off.

The day it began we were staying in London, just for the week. My foster mother, Iserva, wanted to go to an exhibition. Nobody else did.

Because she was Iserva, and got what she wanted, we all trooped along. There was me and Jacob, and Ryan, their son. It was pouring with rain.

The rain dripped down the back of my neck. The pavement was crowded with people and pigeons. I longed to be a pigeon, to fly away, and never come back. It wasn't going to happen. Then we walked through a door, into a hall, and my life changed, just like that. I was staring at a model, Titanic in perspex. It was love at first sight.

Titanic, the model was absolutely huge.

The real Titanic was even bigger, because that's what they wanted, the biggest and the best. The

White Star Line, whose ship she was, wanted their ships to be better than Cunard's. They couldn't be faster, but they could be bigger, and more luxurious. So they built Titanic, and she was the best.

I walked towards the beautiful model and pressed my hands to the sides of the case. A strong steel hull, two hundred portholes, great gold letters, bright, on the side. I'm talking about the real one here. Endless rivets hammered by hand. Titanic was marvellous, and so was this one. I couldn't take my eyes off her. I walked round the case again and again, seeing Titanic from all her angles. I saw my mother lean towards Jacob.

'I've never seen her look like that before.'

Titanic, the model, had four huge funnels. 'The fourth one's fake,' I said to my parents. Then the funnel collapsed and fell to the ground.

Everyone shrieked then laughed, embarrassed, it was all part of the simulation. I just stood there, hands in my pockets. I was shaking inside but nobody noticed.

Later that day we drank stokers' tea in the nautical café. 'How did you know,' Jacob said, 'that the funnel was fake?' I shrugged my shoulders, what could I say? *I read it in a book, we did it at school.* So many answers, but none of them true. I knew, that's all, in the way you know it gets light in the morning. I'd heard about Titanic before, of course, but until that day, she was just a name. Until that point, when I walked through the door.

After that Sunday, I soaked up Titanic like a sponge soaks up water. But I still didn't really remember what happened. Not until later, a lot later.

Several months on, Iserva left. I didn't really like her, and she didn't like me, but she was the closest thing to a mother I had. And her timing wasn't great, the day she left was my tenth birthday.

We were barely speaking by the day in question, but it was still my birthday, and I was hoping for a present, or maybe a card. I didn't get either. But at least this time, although she was angry, it wasn't my fault. Jacob had purchased the wrong wine.

He shouldn't have been buying wine at all, not by then, but Jacob didn't think, he rarely did. And although I didn't say so, I was secretly pleased he'd remembered the date.

I came home from school to find her throwing some things in a bag. Shoes and stockings, blouses and skirts, Iserva wouldn't be seen dead in trousers. The bag she was packing was small and light, she wouldn't last more than a week on that. It cheered me up.

She carried her bag down the stairs and through the lounge into the kitchen. Bras and knickers spilled out the top. Jacob ignored her and carried on reading. He liked to pretend he couldn't care less. Lies, all lies.

'I'm leaving now,' said Iserva firmly. She sounded as if she really meant it.

'Have a nice life,' said Jacob bravely. He didn't look up from behind the paper. Both of us knew she had reason to leave.

She slammed the kitchen door behind her, it rattled and shook. 'Enjoy looking after *her*,' she said. I noticed the kitchen table was bare, she'd taken the wine. It obviously wasn't that bad after all.

I knew what she meant by her final comment. I wasn't forgiven, and never would be.

I also knew she'd gone for good. And on my birthday, the 15th April. Which was also the date Titanic sank.

The irony of that didn't escape me.

4
Lily's Story – 1912

I never believed I'd end up dead, or a ghost of Titanic. I never believed Titanic would sink, nobody did. But she did, and fast, in less than three hours, and we sank with her. Drowned in the ship, what a dreadful end. And all because of my stupid scheme, to get rich quick. Dead, more like.

Lucie and I were at the docks. Titanic towered, high above us. Such a marvellous ship, such a glorious day. I could feel the buzz, the hum of excitement, me and the others, starting again. We were seeking our fortune. I believed it then, I thought I could make it, do anything really. For me *and* Lucie, we were in it together, like we always were. I looked around. No sign of Joss. Typical, that was.

Lucie looked up at the enormous ship. 'Are we really going on that?' she said.

'We really are,' I told her, smiling. If I said I'd had a quiver of doubt, I'd be telling a lie. I looked at the ship and saw our future, mountains of gold, made out of lace and rich people's things. I knew I could steal enough for two. Lucie would help, she'd have to learn. I'd already earned enough for the fare and this was Titanic, not our Southampton, with its mean, tired streets and down at heel folk. I was young and smug and sure of myself.

Lucie just stood there. I think, to be frank, she still missed mother. I skimmed the view, but still no Joss. And no Aunt Maddy. She wouldn't come to see us off.

'I haven't the time,' she'd said bluntly. Maddy sewed clothes, she was always working, huddled away in her tiny corner. But that wasn't it. I knew she was troubled, dreading Joss going, losing her man. For a woman like Mad, a man was everything.

'See you look after the girls,' she'd said. 'Remember they're mine.' She'd looked at Lucie when she made this pronouncement and Joss just laughed.

'I'm sure the girls can look after themselves.' He winked at me, a lazy wink. 'Can't you, Lil?'

'Sure,' I told him, and grinned right back. I knew I'd have no trouble from Joss. Maddy looked worried.

'Don't be fretting, we'll be alright,' Joss said, smiling, putting an arm around my aunt. She looked relieved. But I knew better, I'd seen his face, something was off. And Mad felt guilty, letting us go. Guilty, and troubled. Too many secrets.

Not my problem, I thought to myself. *Not my life.*

But it was, all of it.

5
Carrin's Story – 2001

When I was fifteen, the flashbacks started. Things had changed, and not for the better. We no longer lived in Linsit, for one.

The house in Linsit, on top of the cliffs, belonged to Iserva, it had been passed down to her by the man who built it, her great-grandfather. She didn't want to live in her house anymore, so neither would we. She gave us a month to move out.

I thought, when she left, I'd end up back at the children's home. Instead, we moved in with Jacob's sister, who lived in London. I wasn't that sorry to leave Linsit, I hated the house and all its memories. London didn't turn out to be much better. But I'm talking about the flashbacks here.

Jacob and I were crossing the channel, on a trip to Calais. The weather was lousy and the sea was rough. The wind was spitting rain in my hair. All I could smell and all I could taste, apart from the sea, was Jacob's tobacco. I hated that. So I left him there and crossed the lounge, went to stand by a different railing. I closed my eyes.

The boat was bobbing about in the sea, rising and falling. My stomach fell with it. I could hear people talking, lots of people. That couldn't be right. I was almost alone on a freezing deck. I opened my eyes and blinked, uncertain. It was all different.

The sea was calm, and grey, not blue. There were so many people, all of them grey. The ship was bigger, so much bigger. There were even lifeboats. I blinked again and closed my eyes, opened them quickly. Nothing had changed.

I sat down fast, on a nearby bench. Even the bench was short on colour. I began to feel sick.

'You've lost your hat.' said a woman sharply. She didn't look friendly.

'Excuse me?' I said.

'You've lost your hat. And you don't look well.'

I'm not, I thought, *I'm having delusions.* I pressed my hands, hard, onto the seat, felt its warmth and the point of a splinter. 'I'm fine,' I said. The stranger looked doubtful.

'I'll get you a hat,' she said, abruptly. 'You stay there.' She hurried off, as fast as she could, which wasn't that fast, given her limp. I watched her go. Her skirts were long and grey and coarse.

'I've got to get off,' I thought to myself. I didn't even realise I'd spoken out loud.

You can't,' said a man, walking towards me. 'You're on a ship, you can't get off. And it's a long way down to the sea from here.' He pointed over the edge to prove it. I got up and looked, he was right, it was. I scowled at the man, who stared back boldly. And then he laughed, it lit up his face.

'So where are we going?' I said, bravely.

'New York,' said the man. 'See over there? That's our tender, she's on her way back to Queenstown now. No more Ireland for us, old girl.'

'New York?' I said. I must have looked stunned. I sat back down.

The man confirmed it. 'That's what I said. I hope you're meant to be on this ship. Because I doubt they'd turn round, even for you.' Then he winked and laughed. 'I'm Freddy Stenson, by the way. Pleased to meet you.'

'Carrin Smith,' I said, nodding. 'What did you say this ship was called?'

'I didn't,' he said, squeezing himself on the bench beside me. It wasn't that easy, him being big. I moved along. 'It's called Titanic.'

'And we've just left Queenstown?' My voice sounded faint, even to me.

'Sure,' he said. 'We'll be steaming across the sea for days. It should be fun. Miss Smith, what's the matter?'

He leant across and grabbed my arm, to stop me from falling. As the world around me burst into colour.

6
Lily's Story – 1912

It all went to plan, or so I believed, until she sank. Titanic hit an iceberg, just before midnight. It was dark and cold, and I'd lost Lucie. I was running down the corridor, crazy with fear.

'Lucie!' I screamed. 'Lucie, where are you?' I pushed on the door that led to our cabin; the door fell open. I looked around, there was no-one there, apart from Lee Hern.

'We've got to get out,' I said, gasping. 'The ship's sinking.'

Hern nodded, he was sitting on my bunk, chewing a fag. He didn't seem bothered. I glanced at my feet, a river of water soaked my shoes. The water was rising.

'Where's Lucie?' I said, frantic with worry. 'I sent her back for the bag, ages ago.'

'She was here,' said Hern, 'and then she left. She said she was going back to First to find you. I take it she didn't?'

'No,' I screamed, 'she never arrived. I was there in the room, standing, waiting. She can't have gone back. Where the hell is she?'

'I've no idea, but it's time we left.' Hern stood up.

'I'm not leaving. Not without Lucie.'

'We'll look as we go, we can't stay here, it's getting worse. Come with me, I know a way. But not up at my end, it's flooded up there.'

Then he grabbed my hand and we turned and ran, pushing through people, towards the stairs. We climbed up steps and slipped through doors, ran up and down and wore ourselves out. We didn't find Lucie, and we didn't get out.

As we ran, I heard the voices, the sounds of the people we left behind. They were desperate, these people, shrill and shouting and some of them screamed. But the worst screams of all were the ones in my head, not mine but hers. Lucie alone, lost and frightened, and who knew where.

I knew I'd failed her.

Let no-one tell you Titanic wasn't bad.

It wasn't. It was worse.

7
Carrin's Ghost – 1912

Titanic sank and I, Carrin, was one of the dead, the fifteen hundred. That's a lot of dead people.

You'd think after that, the fall and the death, I might get a rest.

But no, instead, now I'm a ghost at the bottom of the sea, keeping the great ship company. Fantastic.

It's a whole new perspective on 1912.

I stare at the ship, embedded in silt. She's so beautiful. And the right way up, which is just amazing, especially given how far she fell. Two miles down to the ocean floor. It's some distance.

I go for a walk to see what she looks like and get a shock, part of her's missing. I walk a bit further and then I discover she's split in two, bow and stern. Two separate pieces, front and back, with half a mile of sea in between. The stern's all twisted and badly damaged, it's even turned the other way round. My poor ship.

The space in between her isn't just a space, it's a debris field. The first time I cross it I walk very fast. It's a no-man's land of grief and guts, spread all over the ocean floor. I'm so afraid of what I might see. Instead, I focus on Titanic herself, which keeps me calm. I think of the bow, all smooth and cool, not jagged like the stern.

Titanic divided: the bow and the stern. I love both halves, but one breaks my heart. Can a ghost have a heart to break?

Back at the bow, I climb on deck and sit on a bench. It's not the bench where I first met Fred, that one's gone, it was on the stern. So I choose somewhere new but it's not the same. To climb up Titanic I scale the outside, using the ladders, the steps and the railings. I can float if I want, but climbing's better, it seems more respectful. It also gives me time to adjust.

As I climb to the top, I examine my ship. It's not that damaged, not as much as you'd think, although it will be inside. I haven't been there yet, I haven't the nerve.

I wonder what happened to Freddy and Elsa, Elsa's the woman who brought me my hat. We shared a cabin, Elsa and I. I wonder what happened to all the others, especially Brianna. I might be a ghost, but I don't even know who lived and died.

It's dark down here, incredibly dark, but I'm able to see. And there *are* things to see, even down here, at the bottom of the sea. Tiny creatures, and stuff like snow, that swirls up a storm.

Most of the time my vision's perfect. It's very quiet and very dark and there's no-one else, only the shadows that lurk by the ship. They lurk and they wait, making me nervous. The shadows are my only company now.

Apart from Titanic.

8
Carrin's Story – 1996

When Iserva left she didn't go far, just down the hill and across the fields, to the part of Linsit where other people lived. Nobody lived at the top but us. Apart from the woman who ran the guesthouse, Moor House. I'd never even met her.

Iserva never came back to her house. I wasn't surprised. There were too many memories, most of them bad. She soon forgot us, especially Jacob.

Her replacement man was younger and smarter, and a whole lot richer. His name was Harper, Alderney Harper, he was heir to a business. I didn't tell Jacob, he was miserable enough. And then we moved, to live with the aunt.

My aunt's place was a tiny terrace, small and narrow, unlike Babs, who was as huge as a house. There were only two beds and one was a single. That was my aunt's.

'You'll have to sleep with your father,' said Babs. 'I can't.'

I told her I'd sleep with her instead, but she wanted her single and that was that. 'I need my sleep,' she said, insisting. I don't think she wanted to get too close. I knew she'd heard what happened to Ryan.

'Why don't I sleep on the sofa?' I said, with failing hope. But Babs said no.

'What if your father brings someone back?'

I choked back a laugh, but the die was cast. Another bed was the obvious answer, but I didn't bother asking. When Iserva left, Jacob was gutted and lost his job. Now we were poor and living on benefits.

My aunt made it clear she was doing us a favour. Especially in my case, I wasn't even family. Jacob, I presumed, got benefits for me, but I didn't dare ask. I didn't ask much, not after Ryan.

'You'll have to sleep in your father's bed,' my aunt told me. 'It won't be for long,' It lasted six years.

We moved in the spring. Then came winter.

'It's freezing in here, your father's cold, give him a cuddle.'

No! I protested, but only inside.

'It's cold over here, he's missing your mother. Give him a cuddle.'

No, no, no, and she's not my mother!

The nights grew colder.

'Jacob's so lonely, give him a cuddle. Mother wouldn't mind.'

Mother didn't care, Mother had gone. But *I* minded. I shrank away to the edge of the bed, easing my body across the mattress. It wasn't enough. I was pinned in place by a hard, cold wall and a pair of arms.

The winter passed and then two more, and not a lot changed. I went to school and my aunt went to work. Jacob found a job. Then he lost it. There wasn't much demand for small-time managers who didn't want to manage. For a man who was always missing his wife, despite having me. I was just thirteen.

I was quite well developed for my age as well. It must be my fault.

I was costly to raise, clothes and shoes cost money to buy. We didn't have any money. That was my fault.

I was sleeping in his bed, all that temptation, *every* night. The whole damn lot of it, all my fault.

I wanted to die.

No-one threatened me, they didn't need to. Who would believe me and how could they help, even if they did? It was far too late. I couldn't go back to the girl I was, before Ryan, before Iserva, before this.

I hated my aunt. While I was there, I couldn't hate him, so I hated her instead. And Iserva too, for leaving me with him. And for what she did earlier.

After I left, I wrote them off, my mother and the aunt.

I wrote him off too, but that took longer. And Lily's help.

I was just sixteen.

My aunt had a job in a local shop. She chose the job because it was close, she wasn't able to walk much further.

'Now you're sixteen,' she said to me, 'it's time you had a bed of your own. I've saved up the money. Isn't that kind?'

It wasn't kind at all, it was far too late. She bought the bed.

Two weeks later, we won the lottery. Who says life doesn't have the last laugh?

Now we were rich, Jacob gave up looking for work. He could stay at home, as much as he wanted, missing his wife and keeping himself amused with me. Beds weren't the issue any longer. But I wanted freedom. I turned seventeen.

How to escape from a bad marriage? Get a different one.

His name was Rick. He had one thing going for him, he wasn't my father.

Rick was a virgin, unlike me.

'Marry me,' I said to Rick, one night. He had quite nice eyes, and I used my wiles, but he didn't say yes.

'Marry me,' I said, to Rick, one night. 'We can have loads of sex, as much as you want.' His eyes lit up, but he still didn't answer.

'Marry me,' I said. 'My father's loaded. I can get us all the money you want.' Rick looked up, and I saw the yes. The deal was done.

We moved away to the other side of London. Our marriage, if you can call it that, lasted three years. Now *I'm* the virgin. The love virgin.

And I'm scared my father will want me back. Stupid, I know, but the past never leaves you.

Then I met Lily and she gave me a future.

9
Carrin's Story – 2006

When Rick and I split, I moved into a flat. It was all fairly friendly, he got the house. But then I was left with nowhere to live. What if my father wanted me back? He didn't of course, he couldn't be bothered, but I didn't know that. We weren't really speaking. The fear crept in. I needed a place and I couldn't afford to be too fussy.

The flat was dire. The landlord called it a garden flat, and there was a garden, but it was full of weeds. Inside the flat, the rooms smelt stale and the walls were filthy. The paper on the walls was dark red flock. I peeled off a bit, just to see. There were three more layers underneath. None of them were red. Thank God for that.

The flat was rented by two geriatrics. A creepy old man opened the door. He said he'd show me the spare room first. It was full of junk, literally full, right to the ceiling. I couldn't even see the bedroom window. Assuming there was one.

He smiled thinly. 'We'll be clearing this room out before we go.'

Ellie Stevenson

Sure, I thought. Then we walked down the passage and into the bedroom.

The bedroom was normal, apart from the flock. There was also a cat curled up on a chair. I like cats. I wandered across the room to stroke it, then stopped, abruptly. The cat was dead, or rather, stuffed. I left the room quickly.

The lounge was enormous and filled with plants. They looked much the same as the weeds in the garden. The room was warm, it was hard to breath. But it looked ok, it was light and spacious. There was also another cat on the sofa. I didn't go near it.

'You'll be taking those with you?' I said to the wife.

'Yes,' she said, looking rather shifty. I didn't believe her. But I needed a flat and I needed it now.

'I'll take it,' I said, wondering what I thought I was doing.

She beamed out a smile and offered me tea. I didn't accept.

A fortnight later, I moved into the flat. The couple lied, they left the cats. But I ended up keeping them all the same. Lily liked them.

The flat was part of a huge house. It was falling apart around my ears. The cistern was noisy and so were the tenants. Water leaked down from the flat above, not once, but twice. No-one was bothered, not even the landlord. I mopped up the water and dried out the carpet. It didn't recover, nor did the ceiling. It sported a stain and peeling paper, much like the walls.

I used my allowance to pay the rent. Jacob still paid it, even though I'd been married for years. I don't know why, perhaps he felt guilty. I called it my share of the lottery winnings. I saved it all, apart from the portion I gave to Rick. By the time I'd left, I'd saved quite a bit, enough to pay for the rent on a flat. Although not a very good one.

Or perhaps that's all I thought I was worth.

Then I decided to change my bank. Now my allowance would stop for good. Yes, I'd be poor, but I'd also be free. Changing my bank was just an illusion, I knew if he wanted, Jacob could find me. But I told myself, I'd be in charge. Of my own life, to live as I wished.

You can't understand if you haven't been there.

'Try me,' said someone, a voice in the corner.

I looked up abruptly. I was sitting at the table, right by the window. The voice I heard felt more like a whisper, it came with a breeze, a ripple of draught. But it was just before midnight, and the windows were closed.

'You know you want to,' said the voice again, louder this time. And then she laughed.

I jumped up alarmed, and spilt my tea. Another enormous stain on the carpet.

'Who are you?' I screeched at the wall.

'I'm Lily,' she said. 'Why don't we talk? It's good to talk.'

I laughed at that and sat back down, and of course we talked. I needed to talk after all those years.

'I can make things better,' said Lily softly, 'a whole lot better, if you'd like me to.' The air on my neck went cold as she spoke.

I wasn't yet used to making decisions. But it didn't take long.

'Yes,' I said at the empty space where I thought she was. And nodded to confirm it.

10
Lily's Story – 2006

Carrin and I met on Titanic but she won't remember. That was then, in 1912, a long time ago. With six years to go, to 2012. If she remembers, she won't dare ask, we weren't exactly friends on Titanic. Which was how I liked it.

After the shipwreck, after my death, it was cold and dark and not a lot else, nothing to see, including Lucie. I wandered around, looking for my sister. Only, she wasn't my sister after all. When Mother died, she left two letters, the second she told me not to open. Not until I was twenty-one, or maybe, an orphan. After we left Southampton docks, we didn't see much of Joss at all, so I considered we *were* orphans and opened the letter.

Looking back now, I wished I hadn't, all the bad news just spilled out. How Lucie was Maddy's and not my mother's, but because Mad was young, and my mother was married, my mother took Lucie and brought us both up. Maddy had promised never to tell. She kept her word. But I remembered the way she'd looked, stared, at Lucie.

131

Possessive, somehow. And yet she allowed us to sail away, on Titanic.

It wasn't just Maddy who'd lost something. Lucie, my sister, was now a cousin, dispossessed but still my own. It didn't change the way I felt, we'd done everything together. I told Lucie, I knew I had to, even though she'd hate the news.

She didn't say much, she never did. It must have been hard, losing her family, all in a rush. First, my mother, dying in Linsit, then Mad, when we sailed on Titanic, and now me, demoted to a cousin.

'Nothing's changed,' I said firmly. 'You're still my sister in my heart.'

'So why did you tell me?'

It might have not mattered that much to me, but it mattered to her, that was clear. And of course it mattered to Maddy too. I'd seen her face, I'd seen her eyes, Lucie was the daughter she wouldn't acknowledge, even when we lived in her house in Southampton. One of those secrets, the ones that destroy you.

I never mentioned the letter again. Titanic sailed on, and then she sank and I died, and so did Lucie. Years later, I'm still searching, searching the world, the places we knew, looking for Lucie. Maybe Lucie's with Maddy now. Wherever that is.

Titanic changed the way things were. It changed people's lives, changed the world, even for people like Maddy and me. Stories were paused and left unfinished, frozen in time, if not forever. Stories don't end, they just take a detour, to come back later, slightly changed. History continues, warped and distorted but still repeating, until we change it. Which is why I have to find my cousin. It's time to make the circle whole. How do I do it?

There's six years to go to the big anniversary, one hundred years since the big ship sank.

I've started with Carrin, now she's free of Rick and the past. So she thinks.

Carrin was part of the story too, Maddy was angry with Carrin once, for something she did, on Titanic. If I stick with Carrin, I might find Maddy, with Lucie in tow. I've waited for years for Carrin's freedom, for her to be on her own at last, away from those people, Babs and Jacob and cold, cruel Iserva. Now it's happened, now we're talking, there's more I can do to stir things up.

If she'll let me.

Of course she'll let me, she's desperate for guidance. They might even help her, the things I do. Or maybe they won't, but that's not my problem, or my job. My only job is to find my cousin.

I'm nobody's guardian angel now, not even Lucie's.

But I know I can't fail her one more time.

11
Carrin's Story – 2007

A year later and Jacob was dead. He died of a heart attack back in Linsit. I was rather surprised, he was only forty-eight, but I didn't ask questions. It was good to know he'd gone, at last. But I didn't know whether to go to the funeral. My aunt would be there, and so would Iserva. So I sent apologies and went anyway, disguised in a wig and a very short skirt.

'It's a definite improvement,' said Lily bluntly, as we went for the bus. I made a face.

An hour later I was in the churchyard, watching Babs stagger into the church. Iserva was with her, they were arm in arm, like bosom pals. It made me sick. When they came out, Babs was crying. They passed right by me. I tried not to flinch.

'It doesn't seem fair,' said Babs sniffing. 'All that money. She doesn't deserve it.'

I damn well do, I thought to myself. Not that I wouldn't give it all up…

Iserva shrugged. 'Much good will it do her. She was always odd, right from the start. She used to stare, I could feel her eyes on the back of my neck, so I'd turn round quickly, hoping to catch her. I never did.' She sighed and shuddered.

'A stranger's child is always bad news,' said my aunt, with feeling. 'You've no idea what's in the genes.' I shrivelled inside.

'It wouldn't take much,' said a voice in my ear. 'We could start with the aunt, she would be easy. Then there'd only be the blonde one left.'

'Shh!' I hissed and Iserva started. She looked right past me.

'I really did think you'd be more upset,' said Babs to my mother, talking about her brother's death. Iserva shrugged.

'There isn't a lot that upsets me now. All the pain went out of me then, that day in Linsit.' Her voice trembled. My aunt nodded.

'I've nothing inside,' said Iserva calmly, patting the place where her heart should be. 'Nothing for her and nothing for him. I'm sorry Babs, but that's how it is.'

'At least _you_ came to the funeral,' said Babs. 'It's a damn sight more than she ever did. Ashamed to show her face, I'd say.'

My hands curled up, into tight little fists. I stood by the wall and watched them leave. Vanish like Jacob, except that he'd gone, gone forever. A job well done.

Thank you Lily.

12
Carrin's Ghost – 1912

Even before we sailed on Titanic, I knew all about her. She was the biggest, the best, the glossiest ship. Going on Titanic was the chance of a lifetime. I was proud, if nervous, and I meant to enjoy *every* minute. Elsa and I were supposed to sail on the Philadelphia, but the coal strike happened and that was that. What coal there was, was saved for the best and the best was Titanic. The coal was transferred and so were we.

We didn't know then, Titanic would sink. It seemed impossible.

Titanic was huge, ten storeys high. One hundred and seventy-five feet from the keel to the funnel tops. Sixty plus feet, from the waterline to the boat deck. Whichever way you told it, Titanic was big.

But despite all that, she could still sink.

Titanic was a legend, built in Belfast and launched in May, 1911. One year later, on 2nd April 1912, she left Belfast, heading for Southampton. The rest is history.

Titanic left Southampton on 10th April 1912. She was expected in New York a week later, but she never made it. On Monday 15th, at 2.20 in the morning, she sank.

Now Titanic's at the bottom of the sea, and so am I.

There were twenty-two hundred people on board Titanic, two thirds of whom died. If you were a man, or crew, or steerage, your chances weren't good. To put it mildly.

So many dead, so many lost, so why am I the only ghost?

At first I don't mind, there's a lot to see. I float right down to the ocean floor, climb back up, and sit on my bench. I wander around the bow where I can. Then I decide it's time to be brave. I think I'll visit the debris trail.

Titanic's innards, spilt all across the ocean floor. Fragments of lives, spread out like a banquet. I feast my eyes.

Cups and plates and bottles of wine. The wine's all gone.

Equipment and engines, broken and damaged, beyond repair.

A large propeller lies on the floor, covered in silt. I sit on its wings, expect it to move. Of course it doesn't.

The further I go, the harder it gets. There are boots and shoes and children's toys. There's even a dress, it looks like mine. It's a very dark colour, it might be green. I touch it lightly, it feels like serge, my Second Cabin dress. It can't be my dress, but it looks just like it.

I wasn't wearing the dress that night, it could be mine. There are shoes as well, they could be mine too. The clothes have an odour, a sense of loss. It's all so sad. There are other clothes too, strangers' clothes. Where are the people these clothes belonged to, where are their bodies? And where is mine?

All at once I'm very afraid, of what I might see. So I float away, back to Titanic.

Where, strangely enough, I feel safe.

13
Carrin's Story – 2011

Jacob was dead and I was rich, relatively speaking. It was a great fringe benefit. The real benefit was feeling free, being able to do whatever I wanted. Or so I thought. Lily, it seemed, had other ideas.

'You need a career,' said Lil shortly. 'I think it's time you did a degree.'

It sounded ok, so I took her advice and did a degree, in English Literature.

Three years later, I still had the flat and I still had Lil. I'd also acquired a lot more books. I'd made a few friends, but none of them stuck. It was hard to make friends with a ghost around.

'It's hard to have friends with *you* around,' Lily said, shortly. Then she said it was time to move on. 'You need to make plans.'

'I already have,' I told her firmly. 'I thought I might teach, after I've done my PhD, and my Masters. There's a really good course, here in London.'

'There's a better one at Leverhulme. Apply for that.'

'You're joking,' I said. 'Leverhulme's just down the road from Linsit. I'm not going there.'

'You are,' said Lil. 'You owe me, Carrin. Apply for the course.'

She was right, I did. But I thought she was talking about Jacob's death.

'Think of the sea,' said Lily firmly. 'Think of Titanic.'

This made me pause. I hadn't stopped thinking of Titanic, ever. I still had the flashbacks, although that's all they were, short, sharp glimpses, of a face or a room. But they pulled me in.

'Apply for the course,' said Lily, relentless. So to keep her quiet, I did what she said. I also applied for several others, and worked much harder at getting the forms right. But no-one wanted me, apart from Leverhulme.

'I don't think I'll bother,' I said shortly.

'You will,' said Lily, 'unless you'd like me to leave, right now.'

She could have been bluffing, I never knew. But I did know that I wanted her to stay. With Lily around, my life worked. And sometimes, just sometimes, Lil could be fun.

I resisted for a while, as a matter of pride. I told myself, *I* was in charge. But in the end, of course, I gave in.

As she knew I would.

14
Lily's Story – 2011

I knew I was playing a dangerous game. I'd wound Carrin up, tight like a spring. One false move and the spring would snap and the clock would stop, then where would I be? But I had to do it, all the same. She already thought I'd murdered Jacob. I knew better.

Jacob's death was more or less proof. I'd heard about Linsit, about everything that happened when Carrin was a kid, Ryan and the lake. She poured it all out. Then Jacob's death, a few years later, which made me wonder. It sounded like Maddy, Maddy in Linsit, by Carrin's old house. For all I knew, Lucie was with her.

It surprised me to think of Mad being in Linsit, that was *my* home. Mad was from Plymouth and then Southampton. But if she *was* there, she'd have her reasons, Mad always did. She could have been watching Carrin for years, until Ryan died and they moved to London.

Now we were back, or nearly back, Leverhulme wasn't that far from Linsit. I wouldn't try looking for Maddy at first, she'd caused too much trouble, over the years. I'd keep to myself, until I found Lucie. Then I'd see.

I could be wrong, the woman in Linsit, the one Carrin saw, might not be Mad. There was only one way to find out for sure – stir up the pot, and see what happened. So that's what I did.

15
Carrin's Story – 2011

We were on the lawn at Leverhulme Uni. It didn't quite have the ring of London. Or even of Leeds. The autumn term was just beginning, 2011.

'This used to be a college,' I said to Lily. 'And, before that, a mental home.'

'Perfect,' said Lily, a smile in her voice. 'You'll fit in well.'

I didn't reply, just looked around. I guessed by her silence, Lily was too. In all these years I'd never seen her, Lily was just a voice to me. I wasn't even sure if she was there or not, half the time. I thought I knew, but I had been wrong, had found myself talking to an empty room.

'So this is the place?' said Lily then. She was talking about my children's home, the home where I lived before Iserva and Jacob took me to Linsit. Now it was a conference centre.

The campus had changed quite a lot since I'd lived here, but it still had all the Victorian trappings. And the home looked the same, apart from being empty. I felt slightly queasy.

'I thought I'd come back here after Linsit,' I said to Lily. 'After what happened, with Ryan and the lake, and Iserva leaving. But I didn't, as it happened.'

'More's the pity,' said Lily shortly. She sounded distracted. I glanced across at the old front door, with its three stone steps.

'That's where she left me,' I said to Lily.

'So they told you,' Lil said sceptically.

'Why would they lie?'

Lily didn't answer. I think about being a child in a box, there, on that step. 'She'd have waited by the trees until someone came. That's what they did.'

'I bet most of them didn't.'

'I still have the paper she put in the box. I think it's *The Times*. She could be from anywhere.'

'And you learned this, when?'

'When I rang them up, before I got married. Rick was there with me. He sat by the phone, holding my hand.'

Lily said nothing, but I knew she was there.

'The home even gave me my name,' I said. 'My mother left nothing, apart from the box. She rang on the bell then ran away. It was just before midnight, sometime in summer. I'll not find her now.'

'You must have been freezing.'

'She wrapped me in blankets, topped with a jacket. It was blue, and cotton.'

'So she did leave something.'

'The woman on the phone said they threw it away. There was no ID. My mother didn't want me to know who she was.'

'You can't be sure this woman was your mother. The home didn't see her, she could have been anyone. For all you know, she could have been a man.'

'It was a woman's jacket, that's all I know.'

'And they couldn't be bothered to keep it for you? The bastards,' said Lil.

'There was a piece in the paper. I ordered it later, from the newspaper archive. There was even a picture of a baby in a blanket. It was hard to believe that baby was me.'

'I bet you were difficult even then.'

'Piss off, Lily.'

'Why weren't you ever adopted?' she asked. 'Kids your age are normally placed.'

I shrugged and sighed. 'No-one would keep me, I don't know why. It was probably in the file but I never asked to see it. I was lucky to get what I did, on the phone. I think they felt guilty, even then.'

'And damn right too. But I still don't see why no-one would keep you.'

'Iserva told me I used to stare. She also said I followed her around. It was true, I did, I was young and afraid and wanted the company. But I didn't stare, I hadn't the nerve. And why would they think I stared when I didn't?'

Lil didn't answer. Then I got it.

'It was you all along, that's what it was. All this time and I never even realised.'

'No,' said Lily, 'it wasn't me.' But I didn't believe her.

'Now you know why I didn't want to come here. There are too many memories, things I'd like to forget ever happened.'

'You can't run away from the past,' said Lil.

She was right, you can't. I remember the day when I first saw my mother, my real mother, in the garden in Linsit. I can't have been more than four at the most.

I was playing by the lake, in the early afternoon. She appeared, slowly, from behind a tree, it was hard to see with the light from the sun. I stared at the stranger, she was dressed in blue and looked so familiar. In spite of myself, of being a bit scared, I tottered towards her. Then Iserva shouted, called me for lunch. I glanced at the woman, then ran for the house. I looked back once but by then she'd gone. I never saw her again for years.

16
Lily's Story – 1948

It didn't end there, after we died. Titanic wasn't the end of it all. I searched for Lucie, alone for years, and then something happened, unexpected. A whole new life for Lucie and me, back with Mad, in the 1940s. Lucie was living with Mad this time, truly her daughter and I was still the wayward cousin. But at least we were all together again, in the one place, Southampton of course. I thought I could make it better that time. Wrong again.

We were at the docks, waiting to board. This was the day we were leaving England. Lucie had Bart, tight by the hand. Bart was Lucie's little brother and she had him, while I had the bag. There was just the one. It was hard to believe we were really going. And Mad wasn't here to see us off.

I was glad about that.

While we were waiting, I looked around. Everything about the dock seemed huge, from the planks at our feet, to the size of the ship, which towered above us. I could hardly bear to look at the ship, it felt like Titanic all over again. Although the ship itself was quite different.

It won't be the same, I said to myself. *It's 1948, not 1912. History doesn't repeat itself. Much.*

It wasn't just me who was anxious and nervy, Lucie was pacing the dock briskly, wearing out leather, as well as my temper. She'd persuaded herself that Mad would turn up and take us all home. It wasn't going to happen.

'Do you think she'll come?' she said again, for at least the fifth time.

'No,' I said, thinking, *not on your life.* I glanced at the ship, which pulled us towards it. I wasn't even sure I could step on board. Lucie wasn't bothered, she didn't remember her life on Titanic. Just as well.

A tall, blonde girl came running towards us. She didn't see our bag, which I'd just put down, until she kicked it. The bag went flying, unlike the girl. She ground to a halt and retrieved it quickly.

'Sorry!' she said, smiling broadly, and studied the bag. 'Is that all you've got?'

'It's more than enough,' I said curtly, scowling at the stranger. She was something of a looker, apart from being blonde, her hair was curly and her face was warm. Unlike the weather.

'Well sorry again,' said the girl, grinning. Then Lucie interrupted.

'Lil, I've lost Bart!' We turned and looked. He was nowhere in sight. The stranger took charge.

'Don't you move!' she said to Lucie. Then she grabbed my arm and we headed for the ship. Five minutes later, we'd found Lucie's brother. He was right by the gangway and doing his best to sneak on board. 'No you don't,' said the stranger firmly, gripping his arm. He yelled and kicked but he knew he was beaten.

He looked at me. 'She's hurting my elbow.'

'She'll hurt a lot more if you don't shut up.' I glanced at the girl. 'How did you know this was where he'd be?'

'I'm used to boys, I know what they're like. He wanted to go on the big ship.' She grinned at Bart.

'Well he'll have to want, at least for now.' We took him back to where Lucie was waiting, standing alone in a jostling crowd. She looked anxious. We handed Bart over.

'You'll need to hold on to him tightly now,' the stranger warned. Then she turned to me and held out her hand.

'I'm Bess Millar. I'm on my own, my family are dead. Are yours dead too?'

'No,' I said, firmly, looking at Lucie. 'No, they're not.'

Though for all the use Mad was, she might as well be.

17
Carrin's Story – 2011

The woman watched them enter the hall. She smiled to herself, though nobody noticed.

I knew, in time, she was bound to come back. And so, I was right.

With less than a year to the end of time. One hundred years since the ship went down, taking her daughter and niece with it. Lucie and Lil. She'd left it too late to know Lucie properly, but all the same… Blood was blood. Damn Titanic, and damn Carrin Smith. It was all her fault.

And now she meant to have her revenge.

The hall was lovely, polished wood flooring and tall narrow windows. It was also crowded, filled with students. Time for students to meet their tutors, confirm their modules.

'Are we going to be here all day?' Lily complained. For once I said nothing.

I stared at a man with flame-coloured hair, he was holding a clipboard. The man looked familiar, I didn't know why. I walked across and joined the queue, which went on forever. Right at the front, next to his chair, sat a large umbrella. The umbrella was red, bold and bright, much like his hair. We hadn't had any rain since Friday.

'Maritime Studies,' he yelled from the front. He was taut and honed, if a little bit brisk.

'I'd like to sign up.'

'This is for spring, the autumn term's full. Can you wait that long?'

'Of course I can wait,' I said calmly. 'If it's worth waiting for.'

His eyes grazed mine, they were grey, like steel. I stared right back. The man smiled.

'And your name is?'

'Carrin Smith, MA in English.' The man dropped the clipboard.

I picked it up and passed it across, but he looked away. 'How do you spell that?'

I told him the spelling, he wrote it down. 'That's unusual.'

'As far as I know, I'm the only one.'

'That's what I thought.' He went on writing.

'You're Craig Tynmouth, the English tutor.' *And quite a bit older than me,* I thought. Though not that old.

'I am,' said Craig. 'Ships are my thing, ships in books. And your thing is?'

Titanic, I thought, but didn't say. 'I'm looking for something new,' I said.

'Really?' he said. 'Well perhaps you've come to the wrong place.' His eyes were fixed on a spot in the distance. He gave me a leaflet. I took it eagerly.

'Thank you,' I said, feeling unsteady.

I wasn't sure what I was thanking him for.

She watched Carrin Smith walk out of the room, with Lily in tow. *Lily, with Carrin, who'd have believed it?* Mad kept her shields up, just in case, and Lil didn't see her. Mad wasn't pleased with Lily at the moment. She hadn't looked after Lucie well, not on Titanic, or even later. She couldn't bear to think about *later.* But if Lil was here, following Carrin, where was Lucie?

Damn, damn, damn.

All those years, up on the cliffs, watching Carrin, all for nothing. Still no Lucie. Not that Carrin was all about Lucie. There was other stuff too, to do with Titanic, to do with Joss, who'd been her man, at least until that slut came along. The one he married, after Mad. And built the house for, Carrin's house. But Joss and the slut were well dead now, and ha! to that.

Maddy sighed. Carrin was here and Lucie was lost and she had a mission. Two missions really, to find Lucie and deal with Carrin. And no-one at all, not even Lily, would stand in her way.

18
Lily's Story – 1948

Titanic was then, in 1912, but we were about to travel again. To a different place, in a different ship, in a different time. None of it choice. I blamed Mad.

Mad and a woman called Eula Weinhart. She was the one who started it all. I was in the scullery.

Weinhart walked in, she could hardly wait to get off the street and into the house. Not that I blamed her, the drains stank.

It was the third time she'd called in as many weeks. I was watching them through a gap in the door. Mad looked grim.

I was meant to be looking after Bart, the boy, but that was too bad, for once he'd have to fend for himself. Bart was younger, and Maddy's son by her latest conquest. A different father to Lucie's, of course. I was the niece, down from the north.

Weinhart sat on the only chair. Mad was expecting, but never mind that. Not that I knew it, not officially. Lucie had said, but she hadn't meant to. She thought I'd laugh, instead, I cursed, I'd met the father. As it happened, he'd gone.

Leaving us rather short of money.

Weinhart smiled, it looked like an effort. 'Have you thought anymore about what I've said?'

'About what, exactly?' Maddy looked blank. She wasn't going to make it easy for Weinhart.

'About sending the girls and the boy to Australia. It's an outdoor life, and the weather's good. They'll all get trained, learn proper skills that lead to jobs. No more fear of being out of work. They're lucky to get this chance, Mrs Rawlins.'

Maddy coughed and doubled over. She was no more a wife than I was a queen.

'I'm sure you're aware of *all* the benefits,' Weinhart said pointedly, casting her eyes at Maddy's stomach. I blinked in surprise.

How the hell did she know about that?

I could see Maddy thinking, the cogs in her brain going round and round. About how her life could be so much better, just her and the baby. About how she'd have time, and a lot more freedom. *Don't do it,* I thought, but my thoughts were wasted.

'It can't be easy,' said Weinhart slowly. 'A woman on her own, with three children. Apart from whatever… might happen in the future.'

The cow, I thought. *The evil cow.*

'Lucie's got a job,' said Maddy quickly. 'She works in the shop, she's there right now.'

'Oh, no I'm not,' said a voice behind me and there was Lucie, holding some flowers. Today was Mad's birthday, but I'd forgotten, with all the excitement. The flowers looked limp, as if she'd picked them. I turned back to listen.

'That's all to the good,' said Weinhart firmly, 'but it can't be enough. And it's hardly fair on the girl, now is it? We like our children to be young at The Halt, it helps them fit in, but that's not a problem, not for your girls. Lucie and Lily deserve a chance, and so do you.'

She's good, I thought, *she's very good*. I hated her for it.

Weinhart continued. 'The boys particularly, love it out there. They're out in the open air all day. Some of the boys get jobs on farms, and maybe, in time, even their own. If they work hard.'

She smiled at Maddy and my heart sank. I knew her words were taking root. I glared at the bitch from behind the door. She was wearing a scarf on top of her coat. I imagined pulling the scarf tight, watching her face shift from pink to purple. I imagined watching her eyes bulge. I glanced at Lucie.

'Those flowers aren't from the shop,' I said.

'Shh!' said Lucie. 'Maddy will hear you.'

Mad wasn't listening. She was too busy hanging on Weinhart's words.

'I know you want what's best, Mrs Rawlins. Best for the children, and best for you.' Again she glanced at Maddy's stomach. Maddy swayed and grabbed for the door.

'Let her sit down you evil witch!' hissed Lucie sharply.

Weinhart did. She leapt to her feet and pushed the chair across to Maddy.

'Here, Mrs Rawlins, have this chair.'

'While you have the kids?' said Mad faintly. But she still took the seat.

Weinhart was making a move to go. 'Don't think too long, Mrs Rawlins,' she warned. 'There's a ship leaving for Australia soon. The children could be on it, making a start on a brand new life. And so could you. Just think, Mrs Rawlins. But not for too long.'

She walked to the door and stumbled out, weaving her way between toys and weeds as she crossed the yard. She nearly tripped.

'Good riddance!' said Lucie, clutching the flowers. They looked pathetic.

'I think it's time you gave those to Mad.' Lucie ignored me.

'She's going to say yes. Can you believe it?'

I could, unfortunately. Weinhart had left, but I knew she'd be back. I followed Lucie into the lane. 'Never say die,' I said, valiantly.

She turned round to face me. 'Why would I want to go to Australia? Southampton's my home. It's all I know.'

'We could run away,' I offered quietly. 'Just you and me, before she comes back.'

'We can't do that, I can't leave Bart. And what would we live on if we did? Besides, I don't even like you.'

'Fine,' I said. 'It was just a thought.'

'Well, don't bother,' said Lucie, sourly. 'How do we stop her?' She was talking about Weinhart.

'We can't,' I said. 'The only thing we can do is leave, before she comes back.'

'I can't,' said Lucie. 'I can't just go.'

But she would of course, even if only to go on the ship. I reached across to take the flowers. 'I'll give those to Mad.'

'Oh no you won't,' said Lucie then, swinging the flowers out of my reach. 'I'm not that sure she deserves any flowers.' Then she dropped the bundle into the gutter and walked away, getting smaller and smaller, until she'd gone. I stared at the flowers, scattered on the cobbles, they looked, I thought, like a bouquet for the dead.

Which, as it happened, is what they were.

19
Carrin's Story – 2011

I didn't like living in student halls.

'You'll never make friends if you don't live on campus,' Lily insisted.

'Maybe I've had it with making friends.'

She didn't reply, it was one of her tactics, she used it often.

My room was ok, it was in a block for mature students.

'They've got that wrong,' Lily had said.

It was large as well, enough for two. Not that she took up a lot of space.

Then came November, a miserable Sunday. I was trying to read, but no chance of that.

'There's somewhere I need you to go, and soon. Can you write this down?' I did as she asked. It was a set of directions.

'So this is in Leverhulme?'

'It's out towards Linsit. You'll take the road that leads to the sea.'

'So why am I going?'

'Because I say so.' It wasn't enough. I threw the paper into the bin. Sometimes I wished she'd leave me alone. For a day or a week, or maybe forever. No, I didn't mean that.

I picked up my book. The room went quiet.

When I was sure she'd left, I pulled out the paper and took down the details. Then I threw the paper back in the bin. Lily wasn't fooled, but a week went by.

'You can't run away from the past forever,' she said the next Sunday.

'Go away,' I said. 'I'm trying to read.'

The room went cold and a wind appeared. All my papers flew to the floor.

'Alright, alright, what do I do?'

'Just go,' said Lily, 'And don't ask why.' So I did what she said, but first came the dream.

I climbed into bed and fell into sleep, angry and tired. I was standing outside some wrought iron gates. Inside the gates was a gravelled path, it crunched underfoot. There were trees overhead, huge dark trees that banished the light. The path wound sharply, to the left, to the right, then right once more. I was standing in a clearing. Right up ahead was a box-like house, very modern, in dark red brick. In front of the house, but over to the right, past the front door, were two adjoining garages. I walked to the door and knocked, loudly. Then I woke up.

It put me in a mood for the rest of the morning.

Later that day I went looking for the house, or whatever, for real. Which meant catching the local bus to Linsit. I hadn't been back since 1996. I wasn't going back today, either.

'You can't run away from the past forever.'

Sometimes I wished I could switch her off.

Leverhulme campus was right in the centre. The campus was flat, the town was flat, it was easy to forget that the place itself was littered with hills. As the bus wound through the narrow streets, the view changed, the streets widened, and all at once, we were in the country. Leverhulme, the town, had vanished, for good. The bus dropped me off by a country lane. I checked my notes. This was it.

It wasn't the best day for a walk in nature. It had rained overnight and the lane was damp, leaking its water into my shoes. Every so often I was sprayed with more, from a passing car. Nobody stopped.

At the end of the lane was an open field. A farmer's gate gave access to cars but I climbed the stile. In the middle of the field was some sort of barn, all glass and steel and rich red brick, with seams of grey, running all round it. It was quite something. It was also nothing like the house in my dream. I walked towards it.

When I drew closer, I realised something, the barn was a shop, at least downstairs. There was double-fronted glass with a door in between. The door was closed. I stood outside and peered through the window into a room. There was someone in there, a woman, sewing. She didn't look up.

The sun came out from behind a cloud, and all at once, the woman I saw was framed in the light. I watched her work, her bright red hair draped over a shirt. Masses of curls, glorious colour, fell like rain. I pressed my hands to the front of the glass, as if to get closer. And then I remembered I shouldn't do it. I might be seen.

I looked across to the other window, it was full of dresses. They were beautiful dresses, I wanted to look, but I couldn't keep my eyes from the woman with the hair. Then the sun moved round and she raised her eyes and looked straight at me. I was caught in her gaze, unable to move.

I watched her get up and move to the door. She would open that door, and then another, and then she'd be standing outside with me. I stood there frozen.

At last something shifted, I could move my feet, and I ran from the barn, stumbling almost, across the field and over the stile. I stopped, gasping. Right by the stile was a huge, old tree. I hid beneath it. I leant across, over the fence and into the field, straining and peering, looking at the barn, looking for the woman. The field was still, there was no-one there, not even a bird. I trudged up the lane, both relieved and bereft.

Ship of Haunts: the other Titanic Story is available on Amazon, in print and as an ebook.

www.ingramcontent.com/pod-product-compliance
Lightning Source LLC
Chambersburg PA
CBHW032011170626
46807CB00006B/2744